DANNY ORLIS
AND
LINDA'S NEW MOTHER

DANNY ORLIS

AND

LINDA'S NEW MOTHER

BERNARD PALMER

Danny Orlis and Linda's New Mother
© 2024 by Bernard Palmer
All rights reserved. First edition 1965.
Second edition 2024.

Cover image: Adobe Firefly
Character illustrations: John Ball
Editor: Charlene Miskimen

Aneko Press Youth

www.anekopress.com

Aneko Press, Life Sentence Publishing, and our logos are trademarks of Life Sentence Publishing, Inc.
203 E. Birch Street
P.O. Box 652
Abbotsford, WI 54405

JUVENILE FICTION / Religious / Christian / Action & Adventure
Paperback ISBN: 979-8-88936-018-6
eBook ISBN: 979-8-88936-019-3
10 9 8 7 6 5 4 3 2 1
Available where books are sold

CONTENTS

CHAPTER 1

LINDA WORRIES ABOUT HER FATHER

School nights were busy times at the Danny Orlis house. As soon as the little family had finished dinner, Jim Morgan gathered his books together and went into his room to study. Usually Linda Penner did the same, but on this particular evening she got into her heavy coat and snow boots. Kay Orlis saw that Linda was getting ready to go out and followed her to the front door.

"Where are you going, Linda?"

"It's been almost a week since I've been over to the house to see Daddy," the girl replied. "I thought I'd go and see if he's sick or something."

"I think it would be nice for you to go over and spend an evening with your dad," Kay said. "He's been so lonesome, I know that he'll be anxious to have someone to visit with. But I don't think he's been sick. I talked with him on the phone a day or so ago. He didn't say anything about being sick – or even feeling bad. In fact, I thought he sounded more cheerful than he has for some time."

"I won't be gone too long, Kay. I think I'll be home by eight or eight thirty."

The snow crunched under Linda's feet as she walked slowly across town to the little house where her father lived alone, the little house where both she and Becky had lived from the time they were born until their mother died and they had moved to Danny and Kay's.

Linda crossed the street and went toward town. It hadn't been a lie that she was going over to see her dad. She had been lonesome for him the past few days and had decided that afternoon she would go over and see him. But Jack Ross had brought her home from school that afternoon and had wanted her to go out with him.

"I'm sorry." She dimpled at him. "But I'm going over to see Daddy tonight."

"Now don't give me that stuff."

"It's the truth."

"Fine. I'll take you over there."

"I'll be walking along First Avenue about seven o'clock."

"Seven o'clock?" He laughed teasingly. "And I suppose you think I'll come along and pick you up?"

"Not necessarily." She wrinkled her nose at him. "I only mentioned it because you said you didn't believe me."

"I believe you, all right. In fact, I don't know of anyone else who would want to take you out."

Linda straightened indignantly.

"Don't think you're so smart, Jack Ross – or that you're the only guy who's interested in going out with me. If I want to, I can always get Tom Channing to take me places."

"Him?" His lips curled disdainfully. "The football season's over now. You won't have any use for Tom until next year."

Linda Penner half expected Jack to come along that night as she walked over to her dad's, but he didn't. And, in a way, she was glad. If he had, she would likely have gone riding with him instead of going home to see her dad. And she was lonesome for him. She was just realizing how much she missed him. As she neared the house, her pace quickened.

Linda turned at the corner north of their home. Strange, but the house was dark. And that wasn't normal at all. It wasn't like Dad to be gone on Friday nights. It wasn't like him at all. Fear began to pry at the corners of her mind.

She went up on the porch and tried the door. It wasn't locked, but that meant nothing. Dad seldom locked the house when he left. He always said that if anyone wanted to get in, they'd be able to manage easily enough whether the door was locked or not.

She went into the house and looked around. He wasn't in the kitchen and the basement was dark. Her youthful mouth tightened.

Very deliberately she went to the bedroom. His work clothes were there and his old shoes, but his suit and Sunday shoes were gone.

A sense of relief swept over her, and a smile broke across her face. What was the matter with her, getting so excited and everything? He must have gone to something at church. She should have thought of that!

On the way home Linda just happened to walk by the church where they all attended. She hadn't really planned to. She didn't even realize that she was near the church building until she turned the corner.

She stopped short. The church was dark!

So Dad wasn't there! He wasn't anywhere around!

Her pulse quickened, and concern was etched on her face as she walked through the snow to Danny and Kay's.

When she got home, she went directly to her room and tried to study, but it was almost impossible to get her mind on her lessons. There wasn't anything wrong, she told herself. If there was, she'd have learned about it by this time. In a little town like Fairview, bad news always got around in a hurry. There had to be a simple, logical explanation. Still, she was disturbed – greatly disturbed.

The next two or three days Linda tried to get in touch with her dad on several occasions. A couple of times she walked over to the house, and at least two or three times each evening she called. She could plainly hear the ringing of the phone, but there was no answer.

At last Linda felt she must share her concern with someone. She went into the living room where Kay Orlis was sitting alone and took an easy chair. Kay did not notice her. After a moment or two, Linda spoke. "Kay."

The older girl looked up. "I'm sorry, Linda. I didn't even know you were here."

Hesitating a moment, Linda said, "I'd like to talk to you for a minute – if you've got time." She got up and moved closer to Kay. "Have–have you seen Daddy lately?"

Kay closed the magazine she had been reading and laid it on the end table. "I saw him in church Sunday. Why?"

"I saw him in church, too, but I've been trying and trying to call him, and I haven't been able to catch him home. I just wondered if you'd seen him."

Kay shook her head. "Come to think of it, I haven't seen him for a couple of weeks, except at church. And neither Danny nor I got a chance to talk to him there." There was a short silence. "Maybe he's been out on the road more lately. His employer might have given him a new route or some extra work that keeps him away from home longer than before."

"He always used to tell me things like that when they happened." The corners of Linda's mouth twitched nervously. "It's just not like Daddy not to let me know if he's had any changes in his job or that sort of thing." She took a deep breath. "Maybe he's sick or something."

"I'm sure it isn't anything like that."

Linda leaned forward uneasily. "But why would he be gone every night?"

"I don't know, Linda," Kay replied. "But when you get to talk to him, I'm sure you'll find a good and very logical reason for it. Don't be so concerned. Everything's all right."

Linda's small hands moved nervously. "I wish I could be as sure that Daddy is all right as you are, Kay."

Kay went over and sat beside her. "You know, Linda," she said softly, "when I have a problem that's bothering me, I've found that it's best to take it to the Lord and leave it there."

The girl's body straightened slightly and her lips parted, but she didn't speak.

"Would you like to have me pray with you?" Kay went on, gently.

Linda shook her head. What good would it do for her to pray? The thought stabbed into her heart like a poisoned barb. She wasn't a Christian. She had no claim on God for anything.

Slowly she got to her feet.

"I–I think you must be right, Kay. If something had happened–to-to Daddy, we would have heard about it. There's no reason for me to get so upset." With that she turned and went into her room.

Standing beside her desk, she picked up her Bible and held it thoughtfully. Ask and you shall receive, the Book said. But how could she ask? God wouldn't hear her!

Feeling miserable, Linda got into her pajamas and turned out the light. For a long while she stood at the window, staring out across the snow.

If only it didn't cost so much to be a Christian!

* * *

It was the middle of the following week before Linda was able to contact her father by phone. She squealed excitedly when he answered. "Oh, Daddy! I'm so glad to talk to you. Are–are you all right?"

"All right? Sure, I'm all right. Why?"

"I've been trying and trying to get you," she explained. "I've been over to the house half a dozen times to see if you were home and I've phoned – I don't know how many times. But I've never been able to get you. I thought maybe you were hurt or sick or something."

Mr. Penner coughed and cleared his throat. "As a matter of fact, Linda," he said, "I've never felt better."

"Where've you been? Nobody has seen you or anything."

"I–I've been wanting to talk to you about that, Linda." He paused and then asked, "Are you going to be home tonight? If you are, I think I'll drive over."

The relief Linda felt showed on her face. Turning to Kay, she exclaimed, "I finally got to talk to Daddy. He isn't sick or anything."

Kay smiled. "I was sure he was all right, but I'm glad you got to talk to him."

Linda stood by the window, thinking. Her dad was all right – or was he? She had detected something strange in his voice, a tone she had never heard before. Absentmindedly she pulled at the lobe of her ear. Kay Orlis watched Linda for a few minutes, and then went to where she was standing.

"You said everything is all right with your father, didn't you?"

Linda turned to face Kay. "He said he was okay, and he sounded as though he's okay, but–"

"I'm sure everything is all right, then," Kay assured her.

"I wouldn't worry about it only–only he said that he had to see me right away. Tonight. And he talked as if it were terribly important."

CHAPTER 2

A MARRIAGE ANNOUNCEMENT

Linda hadn't thought that her dad would come so quickly, but they were still standing at the window, talking, when he pulled up in front of the house. She hurried to the door and kissed him impulsively.

"Hello, Daddy."

"Say, now," he exclaimed, "that's quite a greeting!"

"Come on in. It's cold out here."

Henry Penner hesitated.

"I–I thought maybe we could go for a little ride – just you and me."

She eyed him curiously.

"If–if that's what you want, Daddy," she said, "it's all right with me. Just a minute. I'll get my coat."

He had such a strange look in his eyes – a nervous, apprehensive look that she had never seen before.

He said no more until they got into the car together.

"Well, Linda, where do you want to go?"

Her dark eyes searched his face. "I don't care where we go, or what we do. I just want to talk to you. What has happened, Daddy? Is there something wrong?"

A tight little smile lighted his face briefly before nervousness chased it away. "Let me get this old car under way," he began slowly, as though he had to be careful with words, "and I'll tell you." He released the brake and started forward. "No, Linda, there's nothing wrong. In fact, maybe things are very right for the first time in a long, long while."

Linda, her slight young body straight as a ramrod, turned to face him.

"Wh-wh-what do you mean?" she demanded.

"I've been doing a lot of thinking and planning these past few weeks, Linda. How would you and Becky like to come back home to live and have things just the way they used to be?"

For an instant she looked bewildered, as though she dared not believe what she had heard.

"Do you mean it?" she asked breathlessly.

"That's what we've been thinking about."

"That would be wonderful," she exclaimed, with a new light in her face.

He sighed his relief. "I knew you'd feel that way. I told Elsie she wouldn't have to worry about you girls. I told her that you would understand."

Linda became silent. Her lips were set, and the color faded from her cheeks. "Elsie?" she asked. "Who's Elsie?"

Henry Penner almost stopped, and he glanced in her direction apprehensively.

"Elsie is a lovely Christian woman I've been seeing, Linda," he told her. "She's finally promised to marry me."

The silence was overwhelming.

Linda froze. She was motionless except for her hands. Resting on her lap, they worked spasmodically. It was a minute or two before she could speak, and then the words rasped out. "Oh, Daddy!" she cried. "You couldn't!"

Mr. Penner eyed his oldest daughter helplessly. "I thought that you'd be happy at the chance to get back home," he said. "I thought you wanted to have our family together again."

Linda's lips trembled uncertainly, and she fought for self-control. "I would," she told him, icily. "But not *that* way."

Henry reached over and touched her arm. "I know how you feel, Linda, but that's just because you don't know Elsie. You'll love her when you get to know her. You'll love her as much as I do."

"Love!" Linda's lips curled bitterly about the word. "You don't even know what it means!"

He recoiled slightly, but when he spoke, his mouth was grim and stern. "You're talking about something you don't understand at all." He expelled his breath with exasperation. "You might just as well get used to the idea, Linda. Elsie and I love each other, and we're going to be married. It doesn't make any difference whether you like the idea or not."

Linda started to cry. "That's the way it always has been," she sobbed. "You don't care about me. You never have. You put me over to Danny and Kay's when you knew I didn't want to go there."

"That was for your own good," he said. "I put you there so you'd have a Christian woman to look after you and Becky."

"That's what you tell everybody," Linda retorted indignantly, "but you can't fool me. I know better. You got us out of the house because you didn't want Becky and me around to see what you were doing. You wanted to have an *affair* with this–this Elsie, whatever her name is. That's why you wanted us out of the way."

Henry Penner broke in sharply, "Linda! That's enough! I can't permit you to talk to me that way! I can't permit you to talk about Elsie that way! She's a lovely Christian woman and was a close friend of your mother's before we were married. I will be very proud to take a woman like Elsie as my wife. And you should be proud to have her as a mother."

Linda had never heard her father so angry. She wiped her eyes and quietly said, "Take me home."

"Linda!" His voice caught helplessly.

"Please, Daddy," she repeated. "Just take me home."

When he stopped before the Orlis house she got out in silence, leaving the car door ajar, and shuffled dejectedly up the walk. When she came into the house, Kay Orlis looked up from her reading. "Oh, it's you, Linda. I didn't think you would be home so early."

The girl stood motionless just inside the door, her thin face pallid and drawn.

Kay put aside her book and quickly got to her feet. "Linda!" she exclaimed. "Whatever's the matter? Is there something wrong?"

"Oh, no!" she replied bitterly, while scalding tears brimmed in her eyes. "Everything's right. According to Dad, everything's just wonderful!"

"What happened, Linda?" she persisted. "What did he tell you?"

The girl's entire being seemed to tremble.

"It–it–" She swallowed hard. "It's what he's going to do that counts. He just informed me that he–he's going to get married again."

"I think that's very nice," Kay said, a smile playing on her lips. "Your dad has been very lonely since your mother died. I'm sure he'll be much happier than he has been."

Linda's voice faltered, and it was all she could do to go on.

"He wouldn't have to be lonely if he didn't want to. He could have Becky and me at home with him right now. But, no! He doesn't think enough of us to let us live with him. He had to stick us over here with you so we won't get in his way."

Kay walked over to the girl, understanding in her eyes. "I know how you feel," she said, "But your dad was thinking of you girls when he had you stay with Danny and me, Linda. He wanted you to have good Christian supervision. I'm sure you'll agree with that if you'll be honest about it."

"That's what he said, but he can't fool me! I know better. He doesn't care anything for Becky and me at all!"

Kay spoke up quickly. "That isn't true, Linda. You know it isn't true."

"If he loved me, he–he wouldn't be wanting to introduce me to this Elsie person," she continued. "He wouldn't be thinking about getting married again."

"I'm sure that Elsie is a very lovely person, Linda," Kay went on, "or your father wouldn't be interested in her. Why don't you meet her with an open mind and give her a chance to show you what she is like?"

Linda's eyes blazed defiantly. "You can stick up for her if you want to, but I'm not going to have someone come in and take *my* mother's place. I'll run away, first!"

* * *

The following evening Mr. Penner came to the Orlis home with his fiancée and asked for the girls. Linda, who was still in the kitchen, turned to Kay and muttered, "I don't care what Daddy says. I'm not going out there."

"But Linda, your dad has come to see you."

She tossed her head in defiance. "I'm not going out and talk to him as long as *she's* with him."

Mr. Penner came to the kitchen door. "Linda," he said softly.

As their eyes met, she demanded, "Why did you have to bring *her* here?"

"I want you to meet Elsie. I–I want you to see what a fine Christian woman she is."

Bitterness twisted the girl's face. "You didn't have to bring her over here to see me. You're the one who wants to marry her. Go ahead. Do as you please. You don't care what I think, anyway."

Firmly Mr. Penner took his daughter by the arm. "Linda, I'm not going to ask you again. Come in and meet Elsie."

Reluctantly Linda allowed herself to be guided to the living room.

Elsie Graham got to her feet and, smiling pleasantly, took a step or two toward Linda. She was a small, attractive woman with a sprinkling of gray in her dark hair. "You must be Linda," she said gently.

The girl did not answer.

"Your dad has told me so much about you. I've been anxious to get to know you."

Linda's eyes flashed, and she ignored the outstretched hand.

Her father's face clouded. "Linda," he said sharply, "you haven't spoken to Elsie."

"Hello." The girl's voice reflected her resentment.

Elsie Graham's expression did not change. If Linda had hurt her, she gave no sign. Her smile widened, and she made a slight gesture toward the sofa. "There's no need for us to stand," she said. "Why don't we sit down?"

The girl did not move. Her features were frozen, taut, and expressionless. "If it's all the same to you, I'd just as soon stand."

There was a short silence.

"I've been so anxious to make friends with you, Linda," the older woman continued. "Did your dad tell you that we are going to be married soon?"

Linda's thin lips trembled. "He told me, all right," she retorted. "Just as though I'm supposed to be happy about it."

Elsie's voice was gentle and gracious in spite of the girl's obvious belligerence. "We hoped that you *would* be."

Linda's cheeks became ashen, and anger fired her black eyes. "Well, I'm not happy about it, and you might just as well know it now as later! You're never going to take my mother's place with me! I can tell you that much right now!"

After a brief, agonizing silence, Mr. Penner started to speak, but paused helplessly. It was Elsie who finally broke the silence. "No one can ever take your mother's place in your life, Linda," she said understandingly. "I wouldn't even try. But I would like to make friends with you and Becky. I'd like to help furnish a home for you and to have you love me as I love you."

Mr. Penner broke in. "You always said that you wanted us to have our own home again, Linda," he said. "We'll have that as soon as Elsie and I are married. You can come back and live with us again."

Tears trembled on Linda's eyelashes. "But–but that's not the way I wanted it!" she exclaimed, almost tearfully. "I wanted you and me and Becky to be together. I don't want *her* sticking in!" With that the floodgates burst, and Linda started to sob uncontrollably. "Go on! Get married if that's what you want! But leave me alone! I–I never want to see you again!"

With that Linda whirled and stormed into her room, slamming the door. Henry Penner and Elsie Graham stood in stunned silence, saddened by Linda's outburst.

* * *

The following morning Kay got up a little earlier than usual and was sitting at the kitchen window, looking out at the storm that was raging outside when Linda came up beside her. "This is a terrible storm, isn't it, Kay?"

"I think it's beginning to let up a little, now." Kay turned back to the kitchen table. "And what would you like to eat for breakfast?"

Linda's lower lip trembled, and when she spoke her voice was so weak and quavering that Kay had to ask her to repeat what she had said. "I don't care whether I ever get anything to eat or not," Linda said bitterly.

Kay's voice was singularly unsympathetic. "You'll get awfully hungry if you don't."

It was a full minute before Linda could bring herself to look up. When she did, Kay saw that her eyes were red from crying.

"I get so mad every time I think about Daddy and that–that Elsie Graham!" Linda snorted. "You know what he wants to do? He wants to marry her and take us home with the two of them!"

"I think that's a wonderful idea, Linda," Kay answered. "It will give you and Becky a real home, and you'll be with your father. We've enjoyed having you with us, but you'll be so much happier living at home with them."

Linda swallowed hard. "He doesn't want *us!*"

"Yes, he does, Linda," Kay countered. "Your dad hasn't been happy living apart from you. He's been a very lonesome man. When he and Elsie are married, the first thing he'll want to do is to take you girls home to live with them."

Linda's attractive young face clouded. "He may have Becky at home, but he won't have me! That's for sure. I'm not going back home to live as long as *Elsie's* there! They might just as well know that right now!"

"That's being very selfish, Linda." Before the girl could reply, the phone rang, and Kay answered it. "Linda, it's for you."

The girl eyed her suspiciously. "Who is it?" she asked.

"It's for you." Kay thrust the phone into Linda's reluctant hand.

"Hello."

The person on the other end of the line said something.

"I don't care!" Linda exploded. "I don't want to talk to you!" She hurriedly hung up the phone. For the space of a minute or two Linda stood beside the telephone, her eyes blazing. "I should've known it was Dad!" she exclaimed angrily. "He doesn't need to think he can talk me into changing my mind. I told him what I think. I'm not going to talk to him anymore. If that's the way he wants it, he can just forget about me!"

Kay Orlis approached Linda slowly. When she spoke, her voice was soft and well-controlled but taut with emotion. "I'm ashamed of you, Linda. That's no way for any girl to treat her father!"

Linda's drawn face was ashen, and tears trembled under her long eyelashes. "He doesn't care anything at all about me, or what I want. He's got Elsie Graham now!"

CHAPTER 3

LINDA OPPOSES THE MARRIAGE

Kay and Linda were still in the kitchen some minutes later when the front doorbell rang.

"Linda," Kay asked, "would you mind going to the door for me?"

The younger girl walked through the house and opened the front door. When she saw her father standing there, her lithe young body froze. She started to speak but could not.

Henry Penner gulped. "Linda," he said anxiously, "I had to come over. I just had to see you and–and talk to you."

"There's nothing for us to talk about," she said petulantly. "I've talked to you all I want to." Her defiance surged into her voice and kindled fires in her eyes. "There just isn't anything more to say."

Linda's sudden anger found an answering gleam in her dad's taut face. "It doesn't make any difference whether you want to talk with me or not," he retorted hotly. "I want to talk to you. May I come in, or do you want me to talk to you out here?"

She did not answer but stepped back to allow him to come into the living room. "There just isn't anything for us to talk about, Dad," she said, self-pity welling within her. "Nothing you could say to me would get me to change my mind."

"You may not believe this, Linda, but I didn't come over here to try to get you to change your mind." His lips trembled. "I just came to tell you what you've done."

Her eyes widened, incredulously. "What I've done?" she asked, her voice rising in anger. "You're the one who's done everything that's been done. Dad. You've ruined everything."

He shook his head as though he had difficulty believing what he was hearing. "Until right now I haven't realized just how selfish you are. Do you realize, Linda, that the only person you are thinking about is yourself?"

She started to sniffle.

"Th-th-that's not true, Daddy. I'm thinking of everyone. I'm thinking of Becky and you and–and–and Mom. I want to move back into our little house and be just the way we used to be. I can take care of the cooking, washing and cleaning. I can take Mom's place."

"That's not the point, Linda," he went on. "And that's not what I came over to talk with you about. I just want to tell you that Elsie says she won't marry me as long as your attitude is the way it is. And I'm afraid she means it." Hurt clouded his eyes.

"Then she'll never marry you, Dad!" Linda exploded. "I hate her!" Her lips curled bitterly. "I hate her! I hate her!"

For a moment time seemed to stand still. Then Mr. Penner spoke very slowly. "Linda, it so happens that I love Elsie Graham. I love her very, very much."

When he had gone, Linda stood motionless just inside the door, breathing heavily. Then a faint smile began to tease the corners of her mouth. She was still standing there when Kay came into the room.

"Who was here?"

Slowly Linda turned, and said, "Daddy."

Kay Orlis went over to the couch and sat down, smoothing her dress with her hands. "You look relieved, Linda" she said. "I hope that means that you and your father have gotten your differences worked out."

"We haven't gotten together yet," Linda replied. "But we will." Triumph flared in her dark eyes. "I guess I showed that Elsie Graham a thing or two. I've shown her who Daddy loves the most."

"What do you mean by that?"

Linda's smile broadened. "They're not going to get married after all."

Kay Orlis sought Linda's gaze with her own and held it firmly. The look Linda saw there was disturbing. It was not an angry look, but one of pity. She sat down and crossed and uncrossed her legs nervously.

"Linda," Kay said, "I feel very sorry for you."

"For me? There's no need to feel sorry for me now. Everything's working out just perfect."

"I feel very sorry for you," Kay repeated. "I feel sorry for anyone who is so selfish and vindictive and so lacking in understanding."

The rest of the day dragged by for Linda, endlessly. She should have been happy – triumphantly happy now that her dad and Elsie Graham had broken up. But she wasn't. The ache and shame in her heart continued to grow. She spent most of her time in her room, staring out the window or trying to study. She was still in her room when her younger sister Becky came in to go to bed.

Becky eyed her curiously and asked, "What're you doing, Linda?" Receiving no answer, Becky went over to her sister and looked into her dark eyes, concern flooding her own small face. "What's the matter, Linda?" she asked.

Hurriedly Linda dabbed at her eyes. "Nothing. Nothing at all."

That seemed to satisfy Becky, at least for a time. She went to her closet and got her flannel pajamas. "I'm sleepy. Aren't you going to bed?"

"I–I suppose so," said Linda, turning half around to kick off her shoes. It didn't make any difference to Becky that Daddy wanted to get married. She didn't care at all. Wild, unreasoning anger welled in her heart against Becky for a brief instant. How could she turn against Mom that way? Didn't she have any love for her at all?

Suddenly Becky faced Linda and asked seriously, "You don't like Elsie, do you?"

The older girl's mouth hardened. "Who told you that?"

"I was listening to Danny and Kay when they were talking a little while ago. I heard them say so."

Linda's drawn cheeks flushed with color, and temper flecked her black eyes. "They say a lot of things," she retorted darkly.

"I know you don't like Elsie." Becky's voice was calm and matter-of-fact. "But I do. I think she's nice."

"That's the trouble with you. You just don't know."

Hesitating briefly, Becky continued, "She said I could call her 'Mom' if I wanted to."

Linda whirled, eyes blazing. "Don't you dare call that woman 'Mom,' Becky Penner!" she exploded. "Don't you dare!"

Becky's face clouded questioningly, and a hurt look leaped into her eyes. "Daddy thought it would be all right."

Linda took a long, deep breath. Then she exclaimed, "He doesn't think that now. And besides, you won't have any reason to call her Mom. He isn't going to marry her – ever!"

Becky's lips trembled. "Daddy said he would. He promised!"

Linda stared at her, incredulously. "You mean you want them to get married? You want someone else to take Mom's place?"

Becky eyed her uncertainly. "I–I want to go home and live with Daddy," she said, her voice faltering.

"I want to have a *mother,* Linda. And Elsie is nice. Honest, she is. She's awful nice."

Determination straightened Linda's lithe young body and flashed in her eyes. "You just *think* she's nice. She does that to fool you. Just wait until she marries Daddy – if she ever does. Then you'll find out how mean she is. You'll see, she won't let us do anything!"

Doubt spread across Becky's face. "Daddy wouldn't let her be mean to us," she said loyally.

"There wouldn't be any way he could stop her." With that Linda strode across the room and switched off the light.

All was quiet for a few minutes.

"Linda."

She did not answer.

"Linda."

"What do you want?"

"Aren't you even going to take off your clothes before you go to bed?"

Linda changed into her pajamas and lay silent, her eyes wide open, staring into the darkness. She wasn't being selfish and unreasonable in not wanting her dad to marry Elsie Graham. How would Kay like it if she were in her place? That would be different. And Danny still thought she wasn't a Christian. Her temper flared. That showed the sort of a person he was. He acted like he was so perfect and everything – just as though he didn't go up against what the Bible said himself.

She sat up quietly.

The Bible said, "Thou shalt not judge," but that didn't stop Danny Orlis. She should have gone in and reminded him of that. That's what she should have done. Who did he think he was, saying she wasn't a Christian? She was in church and Sunday school every Sunday. Danny ought to know that. He practically *dragged* her there every week. She was just as good a Christian as he and Kay were.

Was she? Did she really and truly know what it meant to be saved?

A Bible verse came back to her. *The wages of sin is death, but the gift of God is eternal life through Jesus Christ our Lord.* Had she ever put that verse to work in her life? Had she ever really acknowledged the fact that she was a sinner and needed saving? Had she accepted Christ as her personal Savior? The questions, like barbs, speared deeply into her heart.

Sleep came for Linda Penner at last, but it was fitful. And in the middle of the night, she awakened to ponder the matter once more.

It still weighed heavily on her the next day in school as she tried to study during her morning library period. Her history book was open on the table before her, but the words blurred on the page. What was it the Bible said? *For God so loved the world, that he gave his only begotten Son, that whosoever believeth in him should not perish, but have everlasting life.*

She had had to learn that verse in Sunday school once. She supposed everybody knew it. At least everybody in the church where she'd been going knew it. But in one of her Sunday school classes she had learned the next verse, too. She hadn't realized that she remembered it until that very moment. *For God sent not his Son into the world to condemn the world; but that the world through him might be saved.*

Linda had gone to church all her life. She had been carried to Sunday school in her mother's arms the first time she went, and she had a couple of one- and two-year Sunday school attendance pins around home somewhere. But had she ever personally come face to face with the fact that she had to accept Christ as her personal Savior or she was lost?

The bell rang. Wearily Linda closed her book and got to her feet.

Jack Ross came over to where she was standing. "Hi, Linda," he said. "I've been looking all over for you. How about going for a ride with me after school?"

She shook her head numbly. "No, thanks."

"I've just finished fixing up the old clunker. Thought maybe you'd like to go along while I took her out and tried her."

"I'd like to, Jack, but I can't make it tonight. I–I think I'll have to be going home right after school."

"Then I'll take you home. How's that for an offer?"

She shook her head. "I–I would just rather walk." She was close to tears.

He looked at her suspiciously. "What's the matter with you now? Got a crush on somebody else?"

"Jack!" she exclaimed indignantly. "You know better than that."

"Well, that's the way it sounds to me."

"It isn't that at all. I would just rather walk home this afternoon. I–I've got a lot of thinking to do."

Something in her tone had the ring of truth. "Having trouble with the Orlises again?"

"Not exactly."

"If I was your dad, I'd get you away from that pair of religious fanatics. I wouldn't let you stay where you're abused all the time!"

Her lips quivered. "Don't, Jack. Please." Before he could say any more, she turned on her heel and hurried down the hall. He stared after her quizzically.

Linda didn't know why she had treated Jack Ross that way. Now he'd probably never talk with her again. But she just couldn't go riding with him after school today – not when her mind was in such a turmoil.

As soon as school was over, she got her coat and went directly home. Kay Orlis was uptown, and Becky must have stopped off with a friend to play. No one was at home. But Linda didn't care. She was grateful for the opportunity to be alone.

She went into the bedroom to hang up her coat and, without quite realizing what she was doing, she picked up a Bible on the dresser. She went over to the bed and sat down, leafing idly through the Book. She had never been one to read the Bible very much. It bothered her. But that afternoon she opened to one of the Psalms and began to read.

But that wasn't what she needed. That wasn't the sort of thing she had been going over in her mind. With great reluctance she opened the Bible to the third chapter of John and read it slowly, thoughtfully. Then she turned to the book of Romans.

It was different with Linda than with many who weren't Christians. Although she had not trusted Christ as her Savior, she had attended Sunday school all of her life. She had heard message after message from the Word of God, so to her the Bible wasn't a closed book. From the deep recesses of her mind the general location of many verses came back to her.

Romans 3:12 leaped out to taunt her. *They are all gone out of the way, they are together become unprofitable; there is none that doeth good, no, not one.* That verse applied to her. There was no getting away from it. It seared into the very depths of her heart.

And then the twenty-third verse of the same chapter. *For all have sinned, and come short of the glory of God.* Tears came to her eyes as she continued to read.

Romans 4:7 was the next to stand out in bold relief. *Blessed are they whose iniquities are forgiven, and whose sins are covered.*

That was what had to happen in her life. That was what she had to do in order to get the blessing of God. That was what she had to do to be saved!

Linda slipped to her knees beside the bed and,

haltingly, poured out her heart in repentance. "O Lord," she cried, "I've tried to run from You for so long, but now I know You are the One I need." She paused for a short moment and then added, "Please forgive my awful sin and make me all Yours."

For more than a minute Linda was quiet. She could say no more. Then the repentant girl continued her heartfelt confession to her newly found Savior. And a peace she had never known before flooded her soul.

CHAPTER 4

A CHANGE IN LINDA

It was almost six o'clock that evening when Kay Orlis came bustling into the house, her arms loaded with groceries.

"Hello," she sang out, "anybody home?"

Only silence greeted her.

She set the groceries on the table, switched on the light to dispel the growing darkness, and went into the living room.

"Linda," she called, "are you in your room?"

For answer Linda Penner opened the door and stepped out. Her eyes were soft and luminous, and her thin cheeks were wet with tears.

"Linda!" Kay cried. "What's the matter? Is something wrong?"

"No." She managed a little one-sided smile. "No, there's nothing wrong."

Kay went over and put her arm around her. "Something

is wrong, Linda. What is it?" Her eyes narrowed. "Are you crying because of your dad and Elsie Graham?"

The girl shook her head. "No, it's nothing like that."

"Then, what is it?" she persisted.

"I–I don't know if I can even tell you without crying," Linda said, her eyes again filling with tears. "And I don't want to cry."

"Just start at the beginning and tell me what it is.

"There isn't much to tell, Kay." Linda swallowed hard, and a radiant smile burst across her face. "It's just that I–I accepted Christ as my Savior a little while ago."

Kay Orlis's mouth sagged open. Her hands relaxed and dropped to her sides. Astonishment and disbelief kindled twin fires in her eyes.

"You–you don't mean it!" she murmured. "Linda, you're joking!"

"No, I'm not. It's the truth, Kay. I've been reading my Bible and I saw that I–I had to confess my sin and trust Christ as my Savior or I was lost and on my way to hell." She gestured expressively. "All at once I felt that I just had to do it."

Tears spilled from Kay Orlis's eyes and coursed down her cheeks. Tenderly she gathered Linda into her arms. "Oh, Linda, I'm so happy!" she said over and over again. "I'm so happy for you."

By this time they were both crying. Kay's throat caught as she said, "I think this is one of the happiest moments of my life, Linda."

"I know it's the happiest time of mine."

Danny Orlis was away that night, and Jim Morgan was studying with Boyd Patterson. As soon as possible after supper Kay suggested that Becky go to bed so she and Linda could be alone together.

Becky looked up in surprise. "But, Kay," she protested, "It's early. It's awful early. I stay up later than this almost every night."

Kay was unrelenting. "All the more reason why you should go to bed now."

"But I'm not a bit sleepy." She went over to Kay, and looking into her eyes said, appealingly, "Look down in my eyes. You can't see a bit of sleep, can you?"

Kay laughed. "Get along with you. They're just full of sleep."

Becky retreated half a step toward the bedroom. "Does Linda have to go to bed early, too?"

"She'll be coming along after a while."

"Can I stay up until Linda goes to bed?" she persisted. "Can I?"

"Now, Becky, I don't want to hear any more out of you." Kay's voice was stern. "Get undressed and jump into bed."

Defeated, the younger girl went into the bedroom and closed the door. It was not until Kay was sure that Becky was in bed, however, that she turned to Linda. "This is so wonderful, Linda. I still can hardly believe it!"

"I can hardly believe it, either." Linda's smile flickered momentarily on her lips before it died away. "I don't feel much different, Kay. At least I don't feel the way I always thought I would."

"Don't worry about that. You've confessed your sin and have put your trust in the Lord Jesus Christ to save you. That's the important thing. The feeling will come later."

They went over to the couch and sat down. Kay was the first to speak. "I'm terribly ashamed of myself for being surprised that you are saved, Linda," she began. "I should have been expecting it. It's what we've all been praying for."

"I've known for a long time that I had to accept Christ as my Savior – that it is the only way I could ever straighten out the mess I've made of my life. Now I don't know why I fought it so hard." The clock struck eight. Linda waited until the last chime died away. "My life is going to be a lot different than it's ever been before. I know that already."

"I'm sure it will be," Kay went on. "Life is different for all of us after we accept Christ." Deliberately she folded her hands in her lap. "The important thing for us to do is to make a total commitment of our lives to God. Accepting Christ as our Savior is the first step, the starting place. After we have done that, He can work in our lives. He can lead us into the center of His will and lead us into useful lives for Him.

"I–I know," Linda said, nodding. "I've been thinking about that, myself." She looked down at the floor. "I'm going to have to go and see Daddy as soon as I can."

Kay Orlis waited, silently, until Linda spoke again. "I've got to see him and–" It was hard for her to force out the words. "I've got to see him and apologize for the terrible way I treated him."

Kay's smile was genuine. "I'm so glad to hear you say that, Linda," she said. "After a person is saved, it's important to clean the slate – to talk to those you have wronged and ask them for forgiveness."

The younger girl's mouth trembled uncertainly. "It's not going to be easy."

"It never is easy to humble yourself enough to apologize."

After a brief silence, she asked, "Linda, what are you going to do about Elsie Graham?"

The color ebbed from Linda's cheeks. "What do you mean?"

"What are you going to do about your dad and Elsie's marriage? Are you still going to oppose it?"

Hurt flashed across Linda's face. Once or twice she started to answer, but she could not.

Kay continued, "You know, a stand like you took here when they came to talk to you can still make you very miserable."

Their eyes met.

"You don't think I ought to say anything if they decide to get married, do you, Kay?" Linda said hesitantly.

"I don't think you have the right to say a word. You should be thankful that Elsie is a Christian and that you and Becky will have a home where Christ is honored."

Linda took a long, deep breath.

"I know that what you are saying is right, Kay," she admitted with obvious reluctance. "I–I keep telling myself that I didn't do right when I got so nasty to

Elsie. I know that I've got to apologize to her and–and to tell her that I want her to marry Daddy – and that I know they'll be very happy. But I–" Tears flooded her eyes. "But I just can't do it, Kay. I can't have her – or anyone else – come in and take Mom's place!"

When Kay Orlis replied, her voice was soft and understanding. "I know just how you feel, Linda, and what you are going through. I know it's hard for you. But, Linda, this is the best way. Danny and I will be praying that God will give you the grace to accept Elsie and that all of you will be very happy."

Linda was still fighting with herself. She nervously wiped her hand across her moist forehead. It was two or three minutes before her eyes sought Kay's. "I've decided, Kay," she said. "I'm going to talk to Daddy tomorrow. I'm going to tell him that I want him to marry Elsie Graham just as soon as possible and that I want to move back home with them."

Kay's gaze did not waver. "Are you sure that's what you want to do?"

"I'm positive!"

The older girl smiled reassuringly. "You don't know how happy that makes me feel, Linda. That's a decision for which you'll never be sorry."

Linda's smile flashed briefly and faded away. Her lower lip trembled.

"I–I hope not."

That night Linda and Kay sat up much later than usual, talking endlessly about the things of the Lord.

It was almost as though they had never known each other before – as though a sudden bond had sprung up between them. It was midnight when Kay finally thought to look at her watch.

"Oh, my," she exclaimed, "it's twelve o'clock, Linda. We've got to get to bed."

The girl got to her feet but was in no hurry to leave.

"I suppose we should," she admitted reluctantly. "I've got a busy day ahead of me tomorrow, and you've got your work to do. But I don't know whether it will do me any good to go to bed yet or not. I'm not a bit sleepy."

"Neither am I," Kay answered, "but I think we ought to turn in anyway. We've both got a big day tomorrow." At the door to her bedroom, she turned back to her young ward. "I am so happy, Linda," she said again. "It's so wonderful to be able to have real fellowship with you."

Linda kissed her impulsively and went into her bedroom. For the space of a moment or two she looked down at Becky, who was sleeping peacefully. If she could just be like Becky! Her little sister seemed to take whatever came and made the best of it. She didn't worry about anything.

Linda got into bed and stretched luxuriously. She decided she wasn't going to worry any more, either. Now that she had trusted Christ as her Savior, she was going to turn her life over to Him and let Him work things out.

For the first time in a long while she felt good and clean inside.

Tomorrow morning, if she could find her dad,

she was going to talk with him. She was going to apologize for the way she had talked to him and for the terrible way she had treated Elsie.

She would probably have to apologize to Elsie Graham, too. A Christian couldn't talk to a person the way she had talked to Elsie and not make things right.

Linda opened her eyes and sat up.

That wasn't going to be easy, either. She could apologize to her dad without any trouble, but she would have to tell Elsie how sorry she was for the way she had acted, and that she wanted her and Dad to get married – if that was what they wanted. It would be bad enough apologizing to someone she liked, but to Elsie!

She stared into the darkness.

Did she really want them to get married? What would it be like to have someone taking her mother's place in their home? What would it be like to come home from school and find some other woman in the kitchen using her mother's things? Kay could talk about how Elsie Graham wouldn't be taking her mother's place, but Linda knew better. How else could it be? Silently she started to pray again.

It was morning when she finally was able to drift off to sleep. Since it was Saturday, she slept later than usual. When she came to the kitchen, Kay was already there, busily cooking breakfast. She looked up from the stove and smiled. "Good morning, Linda," she said pleasantly. "How are you?" There was a new note of comradeship in her voice.

"All right, I guess."

Kay was bubbling with excitement. "I was so thrilled last night," she continued, "that I don't think I slept at all until after four o'clock. Every time I closed my eyes I could hear your testimony, and it thrilled me so much I couldn't sleep."

The high school girl did not answer immediately. Pulling out a chair she sat down and toyed with the cup before her.

Kay continued, "I'm so anxious to have you talk with your dad, Linda. I'd like to see the look on his face when you tell him that you've trusted Christ as your Savior." She paused. "He's going to be the happiest man in the world when he hears what's happened to you."

Kay's excitement was contagious, and Linda responded brightly, "I decided to go right over to the house this morning and talk with him, that is, if he's at home."

Kay poured steaming cups of hot chocolate and set them on the table. "I think Danny will be almost as thrilled as your dad will be. He's been concerned about you and has been praying and praying for you since you came to live with us."

Linda swallowed hard, and it was difficult for her to speak. "I know," she said. "I used to pretend that I didn't like Danny and that Danny didn't want to have anything to do with me, but in my heart, I knew better. I knew that Danny was praying for me and that you were, too." She breathed deeply.

"All of that is over now, Linda. You'll be building a new life in Christ."

The girl sipped her hot chocolate. "It–it sort of scares me when I think about trying to live up to what a Christian ought to be. I–I don't know whether I'm going to be able to do it or not."

Kay Orlis smiled reassuringly. "You don't have to live a Christian life in your own strength, Linda. None of us can do that. You can call on Christ to help you and know that He will. Then, you'll get help from the kids at school and from the grown-ups at church. You won't have to do it alone, my dear."

Getting to her feet, Linda went over to the phone. "I know all that," she said, "but when I think about trying to live a Christian life, I get so scared I–I don't know what to do." She began to call her home number. "I think I'll call Dad and see if I can talk to him for a little while this morning."

There was no answer at the other end of line.

"Maybe he isn't home," Kay said after a bit.

"I suppose he's over seeing that woman!" Linda exploded, bitterness coloring her voice. Suddenly she caught herself. "I–I suppose he went over to see Elsie Graham," she added lamely.

Linda tried to get in touch with her father several times during the day, but she was unsuccessful. It was not until late afternoon that she learned from one of the other drivers for the dairy that because someone had become sick suddenly her dad had had to make an extra trip that Saturday.

"I think I'll go over and leave Dad a note, Kay," she said. "That way he'll get in touch with me as soon as he gets in."

She left the note at the house asking him to call her as soon as he returned, but he did not call until Sunday morning. Then he called so early that his call got her out of bed. His voice revealed his concern. "I was going to call you last night, Linda," he said, "but it was so late when I got in that I thought it would be best to wait until this morning. Is something wrong?"

"Oh, no," she said, her young voice happy. "Everything is fine. I–I just wanted to talk with you and couldn't get hold of you at the house, so I left the note. Everything's all right."

"If it's something important, I can come over right away."

"You won't have to do that, Daddy. I just want to see you for a little while. I can talk with you this afternoon if–if that would be all right."

"Well," he said, hesitating uneasily, "I'm going over to see Elsie later in the afternoon."

"Would it be all right if I come over to the house right after dinner?"

"I'll drive by and pick you up."

Her lips curled slightly, and for an instant her eyes darkened. "You won't have to bother about that, Daddy," she told him. "I can walk over to the house." When Linda hung up, she turned slowly to face Kay. "I–I don't know what's wrong. Daddy acted as though he didn't care whether I came or not. He acted as though he didn't want to see me."

"I'm sure you must be mistaken about that, Linda. Since he called you this morning just as soon as he got up, he must have been very concerned when he got your note." She put an arm around Linda's shoulders and squeezed her affectionately. "Your dad loves you very, very much, my dear. Don't ever forget that. And he'll show you just how much he loves you when he finds out that you've finally accepted Christ as your Savior."

Linda could scarcely wait to see her father, and she didn't eat much of her dinner. Every time she heard a car she jumped to her feet and ran to the window to see if he was coming.

At one thirty the phone rang.

"Linda," her dad said, "aren't you coming over?"

"I was waiting for you to come over here."

"Guess we got our signals mixed," he said, "I'll be right over."

In a few minutes he drove up, and she dashed out to the car and got in beside him.

"Hello, Daddy."

"How are you, Linda?" His manner was stiff and reserved.

"I–I've got something I want to talk with you about, Daddy," she began.

His expression did not change. "I don't think we

have much to talk about now, Linda. I thought we went over all of that the other day when Elsie and I were here to see you."

"That's what I want to talk to you about." She laid a hand on his arm. "I–I wanted to come over and tell you that night before last I finally quit fighting God and trusted the Lord Jesus Christ as my Savior."

Henry Penner stared at her as though he had great difficulty believing what she had said. "Do–do you really mean that?" he asked incredulously.

With a radiant smile she said, "More than I've ever meant anything else in my whole life."

Mr. Penner tried to speak, but the words would not come.

"And, Daddy," she continued, "I wanted to come over and tell you how terribly sorry I am for the way I talked to you and for the way I treated you and–and Elsie. I'm terribly ashamed. I had no right to criticize either one of you. Will–will you forgive me?"

Henry put his arm around her shoulders tenderly. "Of course, we will."

Linda had to fight to get the next words out. "And–and, Daddy," she blurted, "I–I want you and–and Elsie to get married."

He pulled her close and held her. His eyes filled with tears, and he wasn't ashamed of them for they were tears of joy.

CHAPTER 5

LINDA APOLOGIZES

Although Linda had determined to talk to Elsie Graham and had worked out exactly what she wanted to say, it was several days before she had a good opportunity to talk with the attractive woman her dad was planning to marry. She had thought she might meet Elsie on the street downtown or that her Dad would bring Elsie over to Danny and Kay's. Finally she had to call Elsie personally and tell her that she would like to talk with her.

"I'm so glad you called, Linda," Elsie said, sweetly. "I've been thinking about you so much lately. Is there something I can do for you?"

The girl took a moment to answer. "No," she said. "Not really. I mean, there's nothing that you can do for me. I just want to see you and–and talk to you."

"I'm anxious to talk to you, too," Elsie replied. "Why don't we have dinner together this evening? Then we could have a good, long talk."

"That sounds nice." Linda didn't really want to go out to dinner with Elsie. Not where everyone who saw them together would think about her dad and Elsie Graham planning on getting married. But she couldn't refuse.

Elsie stopped at the Orlis home shortly after six. She wanted to go to the hotel coffee shop, but Linda suggested a small, out-of-the-way place where they wouldn't be so apt to be seen, at least by people who mattered. It was not until they were seated and had given their orders that Elsie Graham opened the conversation.

"Now, Linda," she said, "what do you want to talk to me about?"

The girl moistened her lips with the tip of her tongue. "I–I don't know just how to begin," she said, stumbling uncertainly over the words, "but I–I– Elsie, I'm sorry for the way I acted to you and the things I said to you and to Daddy the other night. Will you please forgive me?"

The older woman smiled warmly. "Of course, I'll forgive you, Linda. I'm glad that you have come to me this way, but you don't have to apologize to me. I understand exactly how you feel."

Linda fought for self-control. "Did Daddy tell you what happened to me the other night?" she asked.

"He told me that you had confessed your sin and had trusted the Lord Jesus Christ as your Savior, Linda."

"I just couldn't go on the way I had been, trying to run my own life and making such a mess of it."

"I don't know of anything in the world you could have done that would have made him any happier. You should have seen him when he came over to the house Sunday afternoon. He was walking on air."

"I'm glad I've finally done something to make him happy," Linda said. "I've sure done enough to cause him concern and heartache."

"That's all over now."

"The thing I feel the worst about is that I talked so terrible about you and–and Daddy getting married. I know he–he loves you and I–I suppose you love him or you wouldn't be going with him."

"That's right."

"I–I want you to marry him!" Linda blurted out.

There! It was out! She had finally forced herself to say it! The words had seared her heart and scaled her lips, but she had said it! She had actually said it!

Elsie reached out, impulsively, and touched her on the arm. "That makes me very happy, Linda," she said. "We could have gone ahead in spite of your protests, but we didn't want to do that. We wanted you to be happy about it, too."

Their eyes met.

"I'll try."

After a short silence, Elsie Graham said, "Thank you, my dear."

"It's not going to be easy," Linda said honestly, "but I'll try. And, with God's help, I will be happy."

"I'm sure you will." Elsie picked up her fork and

turned it in her fingers absentmindedly. "I suppose your dad told you that we will undoubtedly be getting married very soon."

"I sort of figured you would," the girl said. In spite of herself, her voice was numb.

"We aren't going to have a large wedding, but I have been wondering if I could dare ask you something?"

"About what?"

"Could I get you to help me with the wedding plans, Linda?"

The girl's eyes widened. It was a moment or two before she could speak.

"There are so many things that I need someone to help me with," Elsie went on. "And I'd rather have you than anyone else I know."

Incredulity flickered in Linda's young face. "Do you really mean it, Elsie?" she demanded. "Do you really and truly want *me* to help you with plans for the wedding?"

The older woman's smile gave her the answer. "I know you're so busy in school that it's almost an imposition to ask you, Linda. But if you think you can spare the time, I'd rather have you than anyone else. . . . Do you think you can?"

"Help you?" she echoed excitedly. "I'd love to." She leaned forward, her dark eyes sparkling. "I just happened to notice some magazines over in the drugstore the other day with the cleverest ideas for weddings in them. I–I almost wished I was getting married so I could put them to use."

Elsie Graham smiled. "See," she said, "I knew you would have some good ideas, or at least that you would know where to find them." She glanced at her watch. "The drugstore will still be open when we've finished eating, won't it? Why don't we go over there from here and see what we can find?"

Linda was so thrilled with the prospect of helping Elsie plan her wedding that she scarcely knew what she was eating.

They went directly to the drugstore from the cafe, bought the magazines, and spent the rest of the evening in Elsie's house, poring over them and making tentative plans.

"I think we ought to get all the ideas we like," Elsie said, "and clip them from the different magazines. Then we can go over them carefully and decide which ones would fit in best with our plans."

"That sounds like a wonderful idea."

It was almost ten o'clock when Linda finally got back home.

Kay Orlis was waiting for her in the living room. "Apparently everything went all right," Kay said, searching the girl's face carefully.

"It was wonderful!" She swept radiantly into the room. "Kay, you'll never guess what happened tonight! Elsie asked *me* to help her with the wedding!"

"How nice."

"And we've already got most of the plans made. At least we worked out a lot of things." She lowered her voice. "I know that Elsie wants to talk with you about this herself – and I'm sure she will call you in a couple of days, but I just can't wait to tell you. She wants you and Danny to have part in the service, too."

"She does?"

"That's what she said. She wants Becky to be the flower girl, and she'd like to have you and Danny stand up with her and Dad, on account of you're so close in the family. I mean, Becky and I have been living with you and all of that."

"We'll be happy to do whatever she asks us to," Kay replied.

"And that's not all. She wants *me* to be the junior bridesmaid."

"That's nice," Kay answered. "I hadn't even supposed that she would want you girls to have a part in the ceremony."

"Neither had I."

"Elsie is showing herself to be a lovely person, isn't she?" Kay said.

Linda acted as though she hadn't even heard her. "We got a lot of the planning done, but there are so many things involved in getting ready for a wedding that we're going to have to rush if we're going to get everything done. We're going to have to get together tomorrow night, too."

During the next few days Linda Penner found a joy she had never known before, a joy that can come only from trusting in the Lord Jesus Christ.

Regularly, each morning, she read her Bible and prayed before coming out of her room, and she took every opportunity to let other Christians know what had happened to her.

Boyd Patterson was one of the first to hear her testimony. "It's wonderful to be a real Christian, Boyd," she told him voluntarily. "I just didn't know what happiness I could have until–until–"

Boyd Patterson nodded. "I know exactly what you mean. It was the same way with me before I accepted the Lord as my Savior. I thought that I was having so much fun I wasn't going to turn my life over to anyone. But then I saw that I was just making an awful mess trying to run things on my own. After I accepted Christ as my Savior I found out that my old life was nothing compared to the joy I had as a believer. Now, I can't understand why I fooled around so long before I accepted Christ."

Linda sighed deeply. "If only all the kids in school could have the same happiness and joy that–that we have! Wouldn't that be wonderful, Boyd?"

"You can say that again," he retorted.

At that moment Robin Evans came down the corridor. Boyd took a few steps up the hall to meet her. "Hi, Robin," he said, "have you heard what's happened to Linda?"

The other girl shook her head.

"No, but from the way you're smiling it must have been something nice."

"Oh, it is," Linda broke in. "I'm a Christian now. I've finally gotten things right with God."

Robin's eyes gleamed. "How wonderful!"

"I didn't know how wonderful it could be until after I'd done it," Linda went on. "I've had the warmest, most satisfied feeling since I became a Christian."

The two girls started down the hall together.

"This is so thrilling, Linda," Robin said. "You know, I can tell you about it now. I didn't dare before. But I've been praying for you every day since–since I first got acquainted with you."

"I've found out lately that a lot of people have been praying for me," the other girl said. Her voice cut off sharply and the color spread in her cheeks as she noticed Jack Ross striding down the hall toward her.

"Hi, Linda!" he sang out pleasantly.

"Hello, Jack." In spite of herself, the reluctance in her manner showed through.

He stopped in front of her. "Now, what's with you?"

"Nothing."

"It doesn't sound like 'nothing.' Come on. What's the deal?"

"I–I'm sorry, Jack. I've got to run."

He stepped aside with an elaborate gesture. "I'm sorry I bothered you, Your Royal Highness. I wouldn't want to interfere with the affairs of state."

"Now, Jack!"

"I'll see you later, young lady."

She pushed past him and hurried on, a couple of

steps ahead of Robin. Her friend had to run a few paces to catch up.

"Linda! Don't be in such a hurry!"

"I'm sorry." She lowered her voice as she slowed. "I just didn't want to talk to Jack Ross right now."

Robin turned to eye her quizzically. "Have you said anything to him yet about what happened to you?"

The younger girl shook her head. "Not yet. I–I want to talk to him about it, but I–I can't do it just anywhere. I want to be alone with him when I do."

Robin did not answer immediately, but when she did there was an odd gleam in her eyes. "Sometimes the very hardest thing for a new Christian to do is to let the kids she's been running around with know that things are different with her, that she has given Christ first place in her life."

The color in Linda's cheeks deepened, and she stammered when she spoke. "Oh, I'm going to talk with Jack," she said fervently. "I've already decided that. I just haven't found the right time to do it yet."

That evening after classes, Linda was getting her coat from her locker when Jack Ross came up beside her, a superior little smile playing around the corners of his mouth. "Hi, there," he said. "How's my best girl?"

"I–I thought you'd be gone by now." She stumbled over the words.

"No, I haven't gone." His voice raised irritably. "Maybe you'd like to have me run out so you wouldn't have to face me, but I've been hangin' around to get to talk to you."

She forced a taut, mirthless laugh. "That's fine."

"As a matter of fact, I've been trying to get to talk to you for the past couple of days," he went on, "but you've been givin' me the runaround. What's up, Linda? Have you got a new boyfriend or are you just gettin' tired of good old Jack? What's with you, anyway?"

The corners of her mouth tightened. She knew that the color had faded from her cheeks. "What do you mean?"

"Now, don't try to give me that double talk. You know very well what I mean. Why have you been givin' me the runaround? Why don't you want to see me?"

She gathered up her armload of books. "You're imagining things, Jack. Why wouldn't I want to see you?"

"That's what I'm trying to find out. Just exactly what is it with you? Have you got yourself a new boyfriend or something?"

Her voice rose indignantly. "Jack Ross!" she exclaimed. "You know better than that!"

His bony face clouded. "Well, there's something buggin' you," he said, "and don't try to tell me there isn't. I can see by the way your eyes shine. You look as though you've really fallen hard."

Linda gulped, and her breath came fast. There was no one else in the corridor, and, as late as it was, no one was likely to be coming along. This was exactly the chance she had told Robin Evans she was waiting for.

She could tell Jack that she had become a Christian.

There wasn't anything to stop her. Not a thing. She could tell Jack Ross exactly what had happened to her to put the sparkle in her eyes and make her so happy. She could tell him that she had confessed her sin and put her trust in the Lord Jesus.

Linda turned slowly, only to see derision playing on his petulant face.

"Go ahead, Linda," he said. "I'm waiting patiently. Let's have the big confession."

Savagely she bit her lower lip. An ache welled within her heart.

She knew she should talk to Jack Ross. She knew that she ought to tell him of her newly found faith, even though it would mean that he would ridicule her unmercifully. She knew that she ought to witness to him. But she–she just couldn't!

* * *

Danny and Kay Orlis talked often about Linda and what had happened to her during the last few days.

"It is really wonderful to see the change that's come over her," Danny said, "and to see the way she's going on with the Lord, isn't it, Kay? I know how relieved Henry Penner must be to know that she's a Christian now."

"I'm sure he is. She's been such a problem to him." Kay smiled as she thought about Linda and Becky's father. "And haven't you noticed how much happier he is at church?"

Danny nodded.

"Both Henry and Elsie were very much concerned about Linda's opposition to their marriage," he said. "Her about-face in that area has been a mighty big surprise to me. She's been so headstrong I had begun to wonder if she was ever going to change." Danny leaned back and crossed his legs.

"It's so much better this way," Kay went on. "Now she won't be giving them any trouble. You know, she could have made things terribly hard for both of them."

"You can say that again."

There was a short silence.

"Danny," Kay continued.

"Yes?"

"Have you been thinking that it isn't going to be long until Linda and Becky won't be living with us anymore."

Thoughtfully, he pulled at the lobe of his ear. "I certainly have. I suppose I've thought about that more than anything else during the past few days. It won't be long until just you and I and Jim will be here." He breathed deeply. "Hardly seems right, does it?"

"I can't stand to think of it," she replied. "Oh, I know that the girls belong with Henry and Elsie. I don't mean that. They ought to be with them. That's where they belong. But still, I can't help but feel a little lost."

Danny reached over and put his arm around Kay's shoulder. "It's going to be lonely, that's for sure. I was just sitting here thinking about what my parents went through when I, and then Ron and Roxie left the Angle to go to school. They must have been terribly lonely, too."

CHAPTER 6

VICTORY AND DEFEAT
FOR LINDA

Elsie Graham and Linda Penner continued to work on plans for the wedding. Becky Penner watched the activity with growing curiosity. One evening as her older sister came into their bedroom and began to get ready for bed, she asked, "Where've you been, Linda?"

"Over to see Elsie."

Becky's eyes narrowed. "I thought you didn't like her."

Linda sat down and kicked off her shoes. "Oh, she's all right."

"She's going to be our new mother, isn't she?"

Linda snapped upright. "Don't say that! Don't you *ever* say that!"

"But it's true, isn't it?" Becky persisted. "If she marries Daddy, she'll be our new mother."

"She might marry Daddy," Linda conceded, "but she'll never be our mother! And that's for sure!"

Becky crawled into bed and pulled the covers up around her neck. "She might not be your new mother," she answered, "but she's going to be mine."

Linda got to her feet and switched off the light. For the space of a minute or two she stood there, staring blankly into the darkness.

What Becky said was true. If Elsie Graham married their dad, she was going to be their new mother whether Linda liked it or not. That was what she was accepting when she told Elsie and Dad that she wanted them to get married. Slowly she knelt beside the bed.

Becky raised herself on one elbow. "Linda."

No answer.

"Linda, what are you doing?" Fright edged the girl's voice.

"I–I'm going to pray," she blurted in a half whisper. "I'm going to pray that God will help me to accept Elsie as–as our new mother, the same as you are."

Becky lay back on the bed. "She'll like that."

Linda began to pray, earnestly, that God would remove the bitterness and pain from her heart.

* * *

The next few days Elsie Graham and Linda Penner continued to work on plans for the wedding. They arranged for someone to play the piano and sing and someone to serve at the little reception that would follow the ceremony.

Elsie even took Linda along to help select her wedding dress. Linda found a beautiful white gown that she tried to urge on Elsie, but the older woman rejected it gently.

"I'm afraid it's much too expensive," she said. "Not that I wouldn't love to have a wedding gown like that."

"When I get married that's the sort of a dress I'd like to have," Linda said wistfully.

Elsie smiled tenderly.

"When you get married, I hope you can have a gown exactly like that," she answered.

Elsie chose a dress that was a little more practical – one she could make over after the ceremony. She insisted that Linda select a new dress, too.

"I–I don't know," the girl said hesitantly. "I'm afraid Daddy won't feel that he can get me a new dress right now."

"Oh, but you have to have a new dress for the wedding," Elsie protested. "And so does Becky. He's already told me that he wants both of you to have new dresses. He told me to go with you to pick them out."

It was more fun shopping for a new dress with Elsie than it had been with Kay, Linda thought. Or so it seemed. Elsie laughed a lot and let her buy a dress that was more expensive than anything Kay had ever gotten for her. "Do you think we ought to pay so much for a dress for me, Elsie?" she asked hesitantly, the new dress in her hand.

"Of course," Elsie said, "if you like it. This is a very special dress for a very special occasion, you know."

Linda's face clouded, and she winced. The very thought drove barbs of fear into her heart.

At last the plans for the wedding were completed and the big day arrived. Henry Penner and Elsie Graham were married in the church chapel. Only a few close friends and relatives had been invited. The ceremony was short, simple, and beautiful. There was a brief prelude of piano music, a tender song of faith and love, and the principals came together on the low platform at the front of the chapel.

When the wedding ceremony was over, Elsie and Henry knelt, and the pastor dedicated them and their home to the Lord Jesus Christ. In a few moments the wedding party had formed a reception line.

Linda, somehow managing to look far older than her years, was radiant. "You know, Kay," she said quietly to Kay Orlis, "I think I–I'm almost as happy about all of this as if I were getting married myself." She laughed shortly. "There aren't very many girls who get to take part in their father's wedding. And that's for sure."

Danny and Kay laughed. "We're very happy for all of you," Kay said. "I know that it's going to be best for your dad and for you girls."

Slowly the smile faded from Linda's face. Her lips began to quiver, and her eyes brimmed suddenly with tears.

Kay turned quickly and looked at the girl. "Linda!" she exclaimed.

Without warning a stifled sob broke from the young girl's lips, and she whirled and ran from the room. Everyone saw her. Elsie was the first to act. Quickly she disengaged herself from the group of people with whom she was conversing and came over to Kay. "What's the matter with Linda?" she asked in low tones, concern coloring her voice. "Is she ill?"

Kay hesitated. "No," she said at last. "I don't think there's anything wrong with Linda. I'm sure that she'll be back out in a few minutes."

The bride frowned pensively. "I do hope she's all right," she said.

"I'm sure she's all right, Elsie." Kay touched her on the arm with a slight, pushing gesture. "Why don't you go and join the guests? I'll take care of Linda."

"But if she's ill, I think I ought to go and see her."

"Not this time, Elsie."

Elsie Penner hesitated uncertainly.

"Go on and see your guests," Kay repeated. "Linda will be all right."

Kay thought that Linda would reappear in a moment or two, but she did not. Kay visited with a couple of friends for a few minutes, glancing at her watch every now and then. When Linda still did not come out to rejoin the wedding party, she decided to look for her. At that moment Danny came over to where Kay was, smiling pleasantly. "Hi, Kay," he said, "I've been looking all over for you." He saw the frown on her face. "What is it that upsets you this beautiful evening?"

"I've been concerned about Linda," she replied. "Linda left the others and dashed out the door quite a while ago and hasn't come back yet."

"I wouldn't get so upset about that. She'll be back in a little while."

"But she's already been gone for ten or fifteen minutes, Danny. I only hope that she doesn't do anything that will spoil the day for Henry and Elsie. It's been such a beautiful wedding, and they are so very happy."

Danny Orlis lowered his voice. "What happened to set Linda off that way?" he asked.

Kay shook her head. "I don't know. Linda was talking with me as pleasantly as she ever talked to me. Suddenly her voice choked up, and she burst into tears." After a moment of silence Kay asked, "Think I should find her and talk to her?"

Danny thought for a moment. "No," he said at last. "I don't think so, Kay. This is a situation that young lady is going to have to face herself. It's going to be hard for her, but the sooner that she does it, the better it will be for her and everyone else concerned with her. She needs to be alone so she can take a good, long look at herself."

Kay was reluctant to accept Danny's opinion of Linda and the reasons for her behavior. "It could be that she's just nervous and worked up, Danny," she said. "A lot of things have been happening these past few days – enough to get her bewildered and confused."

"Go and talk with her if you wish, honey," he answered. "I just told you what I think. I wouldn't say that I'm right."

Kay went to the room Linda had entered, but, with her hand on the knob, decided against going in. Almost half an hour later a bright-eyed and smiling Linda came back to join the others. Kay, who had been watching for her, went over to where she was standing. "Do you feel all right now, Linda?" Kay asked softly.

Linda squeezed the older girl's arm. "I feel fine," she said. "I–I'm sorry that I had to go and–and make such a fool of myself, but I couldn't help it. I–" her voice choked once more.

"You didn't make a fool of yourself," Kay assured her. "Everyone was so busy talking that hardly any-one even noticed you were gone."

Before Linda could answer, the photographer came up to her and Kay. "Now if we can get the wedding party together," he said, "I would like to finish tak-ing the pictures."

Henry Penner got Elsie and the others up to the front of the chapel, and the photographer got his pictures. It wasn't long until the refreshments were served and Henry and Elsie Penner had left the church.

Becky turned to Danny. "Now, what are Linda and I going to do?"

"Go home with us, I guess," he said.

Linda swallowed hard and turned away, but not before Kay saw her wipe furtively at her eyes. Kay pretended not to notice, and Danny said, "Get your coats while I get the rest of the cake and the ice cream."

Once back at the little Orlis home, Becky turned once more to Danny. "Danny," she said wistfully, "could you tell me something?"

"Maybe," he replied. "At least I'll try to if I can.

"When is Daddy going to come back home?" she asked.

Danny Orlis pulled at the lobe of his ear. "To tell you the truth, Becky," he said, "I forgot to ask him. But I don't suppose that he and Elsie will be gone for more than a few days." He put his arm around her and hugged her affectionately. "That's all right with you, isn't it?"

Her young face was solemn, and for a moment or two he thought that she was going to cry. "It's all right, I guess," she answered, "but I–I didn't think it would be this way."

"What do you mean?"

"I thought Linda and I would get to go home with Daddy and Elsie – I mean Mom – right tonight."

The lights gleamed in Danny's eyes.

"What's the matter, Becky?" he asked, teasingly. "Don't you like it here with Kay and Jim and me?"

Hurt leaped to her tender eyes. "That's not it, Danny. It's just that I–I'm so excited about getting back home again that I–I can hardly stand it." Her voice broke. "I–I don't want to leave you and Kay. I've just loved it here. But–" Her words were helplessly tangled.

Danny Orlis pulled her close to him. "You don't have to explain to us, Becky," he said tenderly. "We know you love it with us, but we also know you want to be with your daddy. That's the way that it should be." He hugged her once more.

She smiled up at him.

"But," Danny continued, "I'm going to be terribly disappointed if you don't come over to see us real often. We're going to be terribly lonesome without you and Linda around."

"Oh, I'll come over and see you," she said. "I'll come over and visit you every chance I get. I'll prob'ly be over here almost every day – that is, if Mom will let me."

"You come over whenever she'll let you," Danny said. "That will suit us just fine."

Becky left Danny and went over to where her sister was sitting quietly.

"You know, Linda," she said impulsively, "I almost wish we could go over to the house tonight and–and stay there, don't you?"

The older girl's cheeks colored, and it was some time before she could speak.

"I–I don't know," she said. "We'd better wait until Daddy and–and Elsie get back home first before we decide to do anything like that."

Kay, who had been listening to the interchange without saying anything, got to her feet.

"I think it's time for us all to go to bed," she said. "We've had a long, full day, and we're all very tired."

Linda looked up at her appealingly.

"I can go to bed," the girl said, "but I don't think I can sleep at all." The tears came back, quickly, to flood her eyes.

CHAPTER 7

GOING BACK HOME

The next few days seemed to pass quite quickly for Linda Penner. All too quickly, as far as she was concerned. As soon as her dad and his new bride returned to Fairview, she would have to move back home with them.

It wasn't that she didn't want to be back home with Becky and her dad. She had been more lonesome for her dad the past few weeks than she had ever thought she could be.

And she was trying hard to like Elsie. Very hard. She prayed about it every night, and at times she felt she really was going to like her. Still, the thought of moving back home frightened her. It was so-so permanent.

Then, too, she would have to see her dad and Elsie together. Just to think about it seemed to turn her stomach. It was one thing to say that she was going to like Elsie. It was quite another to have to see her and Henry Penner together.

It was entirely different with Becky. The very next morning after the wedding she got up and began to make preparations for moving back home. She got a large cardboard box and a couple of big paper bags from Kay and started packing her things expectantly. Her toys and dolls were waiting just inside the door to her room, ready to be moved. Most of her clothes were packed, too. And all of them would have been had Kay permitted it. Every morning Becky hopped out of bed, rushed to the calendar on the wall, and marked off the number with a crude X.

"There, Linda!" she would exclaim triumphantly. "There's another day gone!"

Linda always shuddered a bit, apprehensively, but did not answer her.

Toward the middle of the week the girls got a long message from the honeymooning couple. Becky, who had gotten home from school earlier than usual that day and had already heard the news, excitedly met Linda at the door. "Oh, Linda," she cried, "guess what!"

Her older sister scowled at her. "Now what is it?"

"I know something you don't!" Her eyes danced.

"If you're going to tell me, tell me. If you're not, just be quiet about it."

"I'm going to tell you, but I'd like to have you guess."

"I don't feel like guessing." She dropped to a chair in the living room.

"Daddy is going to be home in a couple of days," Becky continued.

Linda forced a smile to her lips, as though she were glad her dad and his new wife were coming back to Fairview. "How do you know, Becky?" she asked.

"We got a message today," Becky said. "They wrote that they are both so lonesome for us they can hardly stand it and–"

"I'll bet!" Linda exclaimed, bitterly, curling her lips. "I'll just bet!"

"It's the truth!" Becky retorted. "I can get the message and you can read it for yourself."

"I know they wrote that," Linda admitted. "I just don't think that they care about you and me. They've got each other now!"

"But they said they're lonesome for us," Becky repeated, her lips quivering. "And Daddy never has lied to us."

"I didn't mean it that way," Linda replied. In spite of herself, her pulse quickened. "It will be nice for them to be home, won't it?"

Becky was dancing about her, eyes bright with anticipation. "Before I got up this morning, I prayed and prayed that they would come home real soon. And now they're going to! Just think! We'll get to move back home this weekend. We won't have to stay here anymore." Impulsively she took Linda's hand. "You know, Linda, you ought to do like I'm going to and call Elsie 'Mom.'"

Linda mumbled something or other and went hurrying into the other room. Suddenly she felt numb and cold and very confused. Her dad and Elsie were coming back home, and she was dreading it.

Kay Orlis looked up, smiling.

"Did Becky tell you that you got a message from your parents today?" she asked.

Linda pulled out a chair and sat down.

"She met me at the door to tell me about it. She says that they'll be home in a few days."

"The message is on my phone, Linda," Kay went on. "I didn't want to open it until you got here, but Becky was so anxious to know what they had to say that she wouldn't let me rest until I had read it to her."

The young high schooler shrugged her shoulders indifferently.

"It doesn't matter," she said. "I'm sure there were no secrets in it."

"Here," Kay said, getting it and handing it to her. "It sounds as though they both miss you girls very much."

Linda took the phone and read the message through, thoughtfully. Elsie had written part of it; a long, chatty note that told where they had been and what they had been doing. It was warm, tender and friendly. Remorse welled in Linda's heart as she read. She had no right to get disturbed because of Elsie. As Kay said, Elsie was a lovely Christian woman who would make her dad very happy. She put the message aside at last and looked up. "It sounds as though they'll be back earlier than they expected to be, doesn't it?"

Kay nodded. "That's just what I was thinking."

After a brief silence, Linda said, "Kay, do you think

it would be possible for us to go over and clean the house before they get home?"

Kay Orlis smiled. "How thoughtful of you to think of that, Linda! Yes, I think that would be very nice."

"I think I'll go over and start on it tomorrow evening after school."

Kay looked at her calendar. "I'm supposed to get my hair cut tomorrow after school, but I'll get the appointment changed and go over to the house and help you."

"You will?" The girl's eyes brightened. "I know Dad did the very best he could in trying to keep the house clean. I'm sure that it's not too dirty, but it won't be the way it used to be when Mom was there. And I'd like to have it nice and clean when – they get back home."

Kay put the vacuum cleaner away. "Then it's a date. I'll pick you up at the school tomorrow evening, and we'll go right over to the house. That ought to give us time enough to get most of the work done. And if we don't get finished, we can always go back for an hour the next evening."

The following day Kay put the mops and detergent and dust cloths they needed into the car and went to pick up Linda at school. They went directly to the Penner home and got to work.

Just being back in her home again did something for Linda. "It's going to be nice to start living here again, Kay," she said when they stopped to rest. "I've missed being here much more than I thought I had. I didn't even realize it until this afternoon."

"I'm sure you have," Kay told her. "There just isn't any place like home."

Linda sank thoughtfully into a chair and a strange, pensive look came into her eyes.

"But it is going to be sort of hard to–to see someone else here in Mom's place," she said. There was a long pause. "I've tried to make myself believe that it doesn't make any difference now; that I can welcome Elsie into the house and pretend that it doesn't matter. But it does, Kay. There's no use in kidding myself. It matters a lot."

Sympathetically Kay Orlis came over and put her hand on Linda's shoulder.

"Danny and I have been praying for you, Linda," she said tenderly. "We both know that it's going to be very hard for you. Elsie's aware of that, too. She told me as much the night before she and your father were married."

Linda reached up and squeezed Kay's hand impulsively. She said no more, but her eyes spoke eloquently.

* * *

Friday evening Henry Penner and his bride came home as they had written they would. When he got the suitcases out of the car and brought them in, he stood in the center of the living room for a moment or two, surveying it critically.

"Somebody's been over here doing some cleaning," he said. "I tried to go over things and get the house straightened up before we left, but it sure didn't look the way it does now."

Elsie Penner smiled. "It does look very nice," she said. "And I have a feeling that Linda was over here."

"That's too much to expect."

"No, it isn't," she countered. "Linda's a sweet girl, a very sweet girl. . . . It had to be her, Henry. Who else would have thought of it?"

Henry Penner expelled his breath and said, "You know, Elsie, I still can't get over the change that has come into that girl since she trusted Christ as her Savior. She doesn't even seem like the same kid."

"The change is a very real answer to prayer," she replied. "If Linda had continued the way she was started when you first talked with her about us, I'm afraid that we all would have been in for a lot of trouble. It's so much better now. It makes it easier for all of us."

Elsie took off her coat and hung it in the closet and then asked, "Shouldn't we call the girls now?"

Henry shook his head. "Not right now," he said. "We can call them a little later."

They sat together in the living room for a few minutes, talking in low tones. At last Henry got to his feet and walked to the archway that led to the dining room. "You said something this afternoon about bringing over some of your own furniture. When do you want to do that?"

Elsie was silent for a few moments. Then she replied, "I'd like to get my own things as soon as possible,

Henry, but I'm not at all sure that we ought to bring them here right away."

Questions lighted her husband's eyes. "I don't believe I follow you. If you want some of your own things, why not get them now?" he asked. "What's the point in waiting?"

"I'm not sure how Linda would take it."

His forehead wrinkled. "I don't see what difference that could possibly make to her," he replied. "After all, the furniture is yours. If you want to use it, you ought to be able to do so without any interference from her."

"It's not quite as simple as that," Elsie went on. "Linda has been through a real emotional upheaval these past few days. I'm afraid that if we take out some of your things and bring in mine, she will be apt to feel that I'm trying to take over and wipe out any memories she has of her mother. If she should feel that way, it would hurt her terribly, and I don't want to do that, Henry."

He came back and sat down. "You know, Elsie," he said. "I sure don't understand women."

"What makes you say that?"

"This is one thing I would never have thought of. Have you ever talked with her about it? How do you know that she would feel that way?"

"I've gotten quite well acquainted with her," his bride said, "and I'm quite sure that I'm right. I even think it might make a big difference to me, person-ally, if I were in her place." She smiled briefly. "It isn't a big thing, Henry, but I don't want to do anything that is apt to cause trouble between Linda and me. Things are better between us now, and I want to do everything I can so they will stay that way."

After a while Henry Penner and Elsie went over to the Orlis home to get the girls. Becky, who had been standing at the window since school let out watching for them, ran to them and threw her arms around both of them. "I'm so glad you're home," she cried. "I'm so glad you're home."

Elsie held her close and patted the back of her hand affectionately. "We couldn't stay away from you girls another minute."

After a moment or two Becky pulled free of Elsie's embrace. Concern clouded her eyes. "Are we going to get to go home with you tonight?" she asked uncertainly.

"I should say you are." Elsie's smile faded. "If you want to go home with us tonight, that is. If you'd rather stay here, we can come back for you the first thing in the morning."

Becky hesitated and glanced at Linda. "Oh, we want to go home with you *tonight*. Don't we, Linda?" she asked. "Don't we?" Linda did not answer.

Becky ran over to her dad and clambered up on his lap. "Are you ready to take us home, Daddy? Are you?"

He laughed a little. "Are you sure that you want to go home tonight?" he teased. "Maybe you'd like to stay here for a few more days."

"Want to go home?" Becky echoed. "Why, Linda and I have hardly been able to wait until you got back so we could move home with you. We've been counting and counting and counting the days you would be gone." Sadness dimmed the light in her eyes. "And tonight after supper I–I didn't think you were going to come home today. I thought maybe you were going to stay away longer or something and I–I didn't know whether I could stand it."

She left her dad and, running back to Elsie, climbed up on her lap and threw her arms around her neck. "But you did come home tonight! You did come!" For an instant, words failed her. "And I–I was scared that if you did come back you wouldn't want to take us home with you tonight."

"We wouldn't think of leaving you here, even for tonight," Elsie reassured her. "We've been just as lonesome for you as you've been for us."

After a few minutes of visiting, Henry and Elsie left with the girls. Danny and Kay Orlis stood together at the door after they had gone.

"Do you feel the way I do, Danny?" Kay asked after a time.

"I don't know how you feel," he said, "but I certainly don't feel very well."

She turned back, rubbing her temple with her hand. "It's just not going to be the same around here without Becky and Linda."

Danny put his arm about her shoulder, drawing

her close. "You can say that again." He sighed deeply. "Linda caused us a lot of heartache, but she's a sweet girl in spite of all that. I'm going to miss her."

"So am I. She's especially sweet now that she has accepted Christ as her Savior." A smile lifted the corners of Kay's mouth. "You know, I don't think I've ever seen a change in anyone that has been any more dramatic than the change we've seen in Linda. It really looks as though she's going to go on with Christ in a very wonderful way."

* * *

Linda and Becky Penner put their things in their room at home and hung their clothes in the closet. Becky chattered incessantly while they worked.

"This is going to be just like it used to be, isn't it, Linda?" she asked. "Remember how we used to have this very same room and–and everything?"

Linda nodded.

It was the same in a way, but actually it could never be the same. Not with their mother gone and Elsie trying to take her place.

"Only I'm a lot bigger now than I was then," Becky said. "Elsie – I mean Mom – even said so."

Suddenly, tears smarted in Linda's eyes. And when she spoke her voice was harsh. "Hurry it up, or you'll never get done tonight."

"I will so," she bristled. "I've got just as much done as you have."

A short time later Elsie knocked on the closed door. "May I come in?"

Becky ran to open it. "You don't have to knock to come into our room, Mom," she said. "Just open the door and come in. That's the way I do."

Elsie patted her head lovingly. "Thank you, my dear. But I think it's always a little more polite to knock, don't you?"

Becky's face was serious. "But we don't have to be polite to each other now," she said. "We're related."

Elsie laughed musically. "Don't you think it's about time for you to go to bed? It's getting awfully late, and you'll probably want to get up so early in the morning. We'll have so many things to talk about."

Becky shook her head. "But we've almost got everything unpacked," she said.

"We'll be through in a few minutes, Elsie," Linda put in. "Then we'll go to bed."

Becky eyed her sister reprovingly for calling Elsie by her first name but said nothing. If it bothered the older woman, she gave no sign.

"I'll fix some hot chocolate while you finish so we can have a little snack before we go to bed."

Once the door closed behind her, Becky turned to Linda. "She's nice," she said defensively.

Linda Penner nodded. Elsie was nice. And not just so she could make friends with Linda and Becky and make them like her. She really loved them. Linda breathed deeply. Elsie wanted to be a mother to both of the girls, but Linda found it hard, harder than she had ever thought it could be. A short, wordless prayer for strength escaped her heart.

* * *

Linda Penner found it exciting to be living at home with her dad and Elsie the next few days. It was exciting and a lot of fun. It was good being around him again, hearing his booming laughter, his quiet voice as he read the Bible at their morning devotions and prayed. She had not realized just how much she missed her father until they were back with him once more.

Elsie tried hard to please Linda and Becky. She tried to be very careful to avoid criticizing them or even correcting them, and she cooked foods she knew they both liked.

Becky was so taken with Elsie that she was even reluctant to go to school.

On Monday morning she came into the kitchen in her pajamas. Elsie glanced at the clock. "Becky," she said, "you'd better hurry and get dressed. You'll be late for school."

The girl's young mouth firmed with determination. "I'm not going to school today," she announced firmly.

"Not going?" Elsie echoed.

"I'm not going."

Elsie knelt beside Becky and put an arm about her tenderly. "You don't look sick, honey."

"I–I don't feel so good." Becky's lips quivered.

Her new mother felt her forehead. "I don't think you've got a fever."

Becky hesitated, and said, "I'm not going to school, anyway. I'm going to stay home with you."

Gently, Elsie disengaged Becky's arms from about her neck. "I'd like to have you stay at home with me, Becky," she said, "but that wouldn't be right. You've got to go to school so you can learn. You wouldn't want to grow up not knowing arithmetic and spelling and reading, would you?"

Becky's eyes sparked defiantly. "I wouldn't care."

"Oh, yes, you would." Elsie was gentle but firm. "You think you wouldn't care now, but when you got older, you'd feel terrible. Come on, I'll help you pick out clothes for you to wear today. That is, if you want me to."

Becky took her hand, and they started toward the bedroom door together.

Linda broke in sharply. "That's silly for you to talk about not going to school," she said. "You know that you've got to go."

Her young sister made a face at her. "Nobody was talking to you."

"Now, Becky," Elsie said, disapproval edging her voice. "We don't talk that way to one another."

"I–I'm sorry," Becky said. Then she directed her attention to Elsie once more. "You'll be here when I get home tonight, won't you?"

The older woman nodded. "Of course, I will."

"I'm coming straight home from school. I'll run all the way."

CHAPTER 8

LINDA GETS IN A TIGHT SPOT

Linda Penner had been reading her Bible and praying regularly every morning since she had accepted Christ as her Savior. It seemed to make the day go much better for her. It helped her to get along a little better with Becky and with her dad and Elsie at home.

Linda had not deliberately avoided Jack Ross the past few weeks, but it had been quite some time since she had seen him to talk with him. She was somewhat surprised when he stopped her in the corridor that afternoon and said that he had something to see her about.

"Hi, Kitten," he said brashly, coming up to her as though he owned her. "Where've you been all my life?"

"I've been around." She smiled in greeting.

"I've been turnin' this schoolhouse upside down lookin' for you this afternoon."

"You weren't looking for me in the right places," she said. "I've been around all the time."

He leaned against a locker in front of her. "What've you been doin' lately?" he asked.

"Nothing much." She laughed giddily. Somehow Jack Ross affected her that way. "I haven't been doing much of anything except studying."

"That's not the way I hear it," he continued arrogantly.

Her eyes narrowed and for a moment her pulse quickened. "What have you been hearing?" she asked. "You know that not everything you hear is true."

He laughed. "I don't know whether I even dare to tell you what I've heard about you or not."

"Then it probably isn't true," she retorted. "You know how this school is about talking."

"Yeh, I know." His eyes were laughing at her. "But this story came straight. Straight from a reliable source."

"Now you have got me curious," she said.

He was silent for a moment. "The story I heard came to me straight enough," he said. In that instant the laughter went out of his eyes, and he was very serious. "But I don't think it's true. It couldn't be. I told 'em that it couldn't be true." He straightened and eyed her searchingly. "You haven't 'got religion' like they say, have you?"

Color flooded Linda's thin cheeks, and her lips trembled. "I–I–" she stammered.

His eyes widened incredulously. "Is it true?" he demanded.

"What if it is?"

Jack Ross laughed indulgently. "You sure had me fooled for a minute." He laughed again as he took her by the arm and started down the corridor with her. "You almost had me believin' you'd gone soft in the head or somethin'. You're a great kidder, you are."

Linda's face paled and she glanced his way uneasily. She couldn't go on having him think she wasn't a Christian. She couldn't keep still now after he had said what he had. But she had to tell him the truth. She couldn't keep him from knowing that she was a Christian. What was it that the Bible said about confessing Christ?

While she was framing the words in her mind, he stopped just inside the front door. "I've only got a minute, Linda," he said, "but I did want to talk to you. How about going out with me tomorrow night?"

She hesitated.

"What's the matter, don't you want to?"

"It's not that," she said. "You know it's not anything like that. Only I–I don't know what Elsie would think if I do." She spoke uncertainly.

"What difference does it make what this Elsie person thinks?" he demanded hotly. "You're old enough to know who you want to go out with, aren't you?" He breathed deeply. "Or is it that you just don't want to go with me anymore? Are you looking for a new boyfriend?"

She spoke quickly. "Oh, I always have had a good time with you, Jack," she told him. "You know that."

He grinned possessively, and his old arrogance came back. "Good. Then it's all settled. I'll pick you up at the snack shop at seven thirty tomorrow night."

Before she had an opportunity to reply to him, he went striding away. She stood there, rooted to the spot and staring after him until he disappeared from view. Perspiration came out on her forehead, and she wiped it away with trembling fingers.

Jack Ross wasn't a Christian. He didn't have any use for anything that had to do with "religion" as he called it. And she hadn't said anything to him about her own experience of trusting Christ. She hadn't told him that she was a Christian now. She hadn't denied that she was, but she had masked her faith and let him go away thinking that she didn't love the Lord Jesus Christ. And, what was worse, she had agreed to have another date with him. That, when she knew that a Christian girl should never date a boy who didn't know the Lord as his personal Savior.

Linda left the school and slowly walked home alone. When she reached the house, Elsie was in the kitchen getting supper. "Is that you, Linda?" she called out as the front door opened.

Suddenly, and for no reason at all, Linda's temper flared. "Of course, it's me!" she snapped. "Who'd you expect?"

Elsie came to the door, concern in her eyes. "Linda," she said, "is there something wrong?"

The girl hesitated.

"No." For an instant her lips trembled. "No," she repeated, "there's nothing wrong. Everything's just fine."

She turned on her heel and went into her room.

* * *

Linda Penner was very quiet at the supper table that evening and as soon as the dishes were done and the kitchen straightened, she went to her room. Closing her door, she sat down at the desk, her Bible opened before her.

There were tests in school the next day and she hadn't even begun to review for them, but for the moment she had all but forgotten them. She looked down at her Bible and tried to read, but the words blurred and ran together.

She had failed Christ! That realization stabbed deeply into her heart.

She had talked about witnessing – indeed, she had been praying about it. All along she had known what she should do. Jack Ross was one of the first ones she would have to talk with about the Lord Jesus Christ. Lying on her bed at night she had planned exactly how she would broach the subject to him – just what she would say. She was going to make him see what it was to trust Christ as his Savior. She was going to tell him just how happy she had been since she had become a Christian. But when the time came, she had remained silent. She had denied her faith by not speaking up in as real a way as Peter had denied the Lord, even though he had done it with words.

Linda brushed her hand uneasily across her forehead.

She had been praying and praying that God would give her a good opportunity to witness to Jack. She had prayed that God would help her to have a chance to talk with Jack alone and to get on the subject so she could speak to him about his soul. God had answered her prayer. Jack had even brought up the subject himself, which made it easier for her. And what had she done? She had gotten red and flustered and hadn't been able to say a word! If that wasn't enough, she had agreed to go out with Jack again when she knew that, as a Christian, she had no right to date him. What was the matter with her anyway?

Linda pushed her Bible aside with a quick, nervous gesture and looked off into space. She was still sitting there, motionless, when Becky opened the door and came in quietly. Linda was so absorbed in thought she scarcely heard her.

"Daddy says I have to go to bed now."

Her sister did not answer her.

"I don't see why I have to go to bed first," Becky continued. "It's not fair."

Linda sighed and, closing her Bible, gathered up her books and went into the other room where her dad and Elsie were sitting. Mr. Penner looked up. "Hello, Linda," he said. "I thought probably you were in bed."

She shook her head.

"Is everything all right?" he asked.

"I guess so." She tried desperately to keep the concern from her voice.

"You act as though something is wrong," he insisted.

Her head snapped up, eyes blazing. "How many times do I have to tell you that everything's all right?" she demanded. "Don't you believe what I say?"

"Linda!" Her dad's voice was stern. "That's no way for you to talk to me."

Her sudden anger died. "I–I'm sorry." She sat down and tried to study, but it was useless. Try as she would, she could not get her mind on her lessons, even though she knew she was to have tests the next day. After a time, she gave up and went to her bedroom to get ready for bed. Becky was asleep so she undressed in the darkness. For an hour after she crawled into bed beside her younger sister, she lay on her back, staring up at the ceiling in the darkness. She was weary, but her mind was too active for her to go to sleep.

She had to see Jack Ross just as soon as possible. She had to tell him what had happened to her – that the rumor he had heard about her was true. She had to tell him that she was a Christian now. Yes, she even had to go further than that. She had to tell him that because she was a Christian, she wouldn't be able to date him anymore.

It all seemed so simple as she lay in bed thinking about it. It seemed that it would be easy to find Jack Ross and talk with him about it. She went over in her mind once more just what she would say to Jack, just how she would answer him when he started to ridicule her. If he responded to the gospel, she'd take him to Danny or to the pastor so they could lead him to Christ. And if he didn't, she just wouldn't go out with him anymore. That was all there was to it.

Linda could scarcely wait until morning to see Jack Ross and talk with him about the Savior.

She got to sleep along toward morning, but when her alarm clock rang, she immediately got up and dressed. She hurried to school as soon as she had finished breakfast, approaching the building breathlessly.

If she could just catch Jack Ross at school before class, she would talk to him then. She just had to see him as soon as possible and set the record straight. She had to let him know she was a Christian.

Ordinarily Linda would have been sure of seeing Jack Ross any morning that she wanted to come to school a little early and look around for him. But that particular day he was nowhere to be found. She walked up and down the corridors with studied casualness, for she didn't want anyone to know what she was up to. But, as it turned out, she might just as well have come to school at her usual time. Jack didn't show up.

Linda waited uneasily for noon, hoping to see Jack then, but again she didn't see him. And after school there were two other guys with him when she met him just inside the front door. He looked at her and winked broadly. She signaled to him with her eyes that she wanted to talk to him, but he missed it – or pretended to. At any rate she had no chance of seeing him alone.

Linda got her books and left the school building, disappointment etching her young face. There was nothing for her to do that night except to go to the shop as she had planned and explain everything to Jack there. He'd be alone then. He always said he didn't go much for double dating.

But how could she tell Elsie and her dad where she was planning to go? They wouldn't even let her leave the house if they knew that she was going out on a weeknight to meet a boy. And especially a boy like Jack Ross. Still, she couldn't lie to them. The problem nagged at her. That evening as soon as they had finished supper, she got up and began to clear the table. Her dad noticed it and said jokingly, "Well now, Linda, just what are you planning on doing tonight that you're in such a hurry to get your work done? His face was sober, but laughter twinkled in his eyes.

Linda saw that he was teasing her. Still embarrassment colored her cheeks and she looked quickly away. "I–I have to go uptown, Daddy," she said. "If it's all right with you."

His forehead crinkled. "It's a school night, Linda," he reminded her. "You aren't planning to be gone long, are you?"

She shook her head. "Oh, I won't be gone long," she said. "In fact, I think I will be back home by nine o'clock or before. That isn't too late, is it?"

"I guess not. If you're sure that you will be in by that time."

She finished the dishes and went to get her coat. Becky followed her to the door, talking incessantly.

"Can I go with you?"

"Not tonight."

"Where're you going?"

"Uptown."

"You could take me over to see Danny and Kay, couldn't you?" Becky persisted. "I haven't been over to see them for a long time, and I promised them I would."

"No, I can't take you over to see Danny and Kay," Linda said irritably. "I've got to run, Becky, or I'll be late."

"Who are you going to be with?" Becky called after her.

But Linda closed the door and hurried off the porch without answering.

Although she was supposed to meet Jack Ross at the snack shop at seven thirty, it was almost eight o'clock when he finally came breezing in. Inside the door he stopped and looked around imperiously. Linda got to her feet and motioned to him. He came striding back to where she was standing, regally, as though he was condescending to come over and talk to her. "Hello, Kitten," he said.

"I had just about given you up, Jack," she told him, her irritation apparent in her voice.

He shrugged his shoulders indifferently. "Sorry," he retorted, "but I couldn't make it any sooner. Something came up that I had to take care of. I figured it would be easier for you to wait than for me to put off what I had to do."

Linda turned toward the booth. "Come on and sit down, Jack. I–I'd like to talk with you."

He shook his head. "Can't do it, Kitten. I left the car running. Come on. We'll go out for a spin in my car. It's no fun in a crummy dump like this."

"But–" She started to protest, but Jack paid no attention to it. He headed for the door. "Come on," he said, grabbing her by the arm, "I've got to give you a ride in the old bus before you forget what it's like. It's been forever since you've been out with me."

"It has been a long time," she admitted.

"I'm going to give you a ride that is a ride. I've got the old bus fixed up now! There's not another car in the country that can keep up with her."

He glanced at Linda and frowned. "Now what's got you so worked up?" he asked irritably. "You sure don't seem very excited about going for a ride with me."

"Oh, I am," she countered. "It–it's real exciting."

He beamed at her. "Just you wait till we get out where I can open her up. You'll really flip when I get out on the open road so I can pour on the gas!"

He drove to the end of the block, made a U-turn, and headed for the highway. Linda turned in the seat to look at him. If she could just find words to tell him what she was thinking. If she could just make him understand how much Jesus meant to her – what it was like to be a Christian.

Jack Ross depressed the accelerator, and the finely tuned engine responded with a deep-throated roar.

"Just listen to her!" he exclaimed exultantly. "Just listen to her! Doesn't she take off like a rocket?"

Excitement tingled in the very tips of Linda's fingers.

"Yes, she does!" she exclaimed.

Jack Ross made a face. "Wish I could give you a real ride," he said apologetically, "but I won't be able to open her up tonight. I don't dare."

"Why not?"

"The cops and the highway patrol have really got it in for me now. I can't even drive to school without one of them tailing me. It looks like they've got nothin' to do in this town except to watch what I do. I tell you, Linda, when they get it in for a guy, they never do lay off."

She made no reply. Presently she asked, "Any drag races coming up soon?"

He grinned. "That's the girl who *used* to go with me!" he said exultantly. "Want to see me drive in a few drag races this year?"

Her smile faded. "It's something to do."

"I'm just waitin' for 'em to start this year," he told her. "Just waitin'. I'm goin' to show everybody what I can do this year."

"You sound confident." She giggled.

"You can laugh now, but just you wait," he said. "The first Sunday there's a drag race, I'll take you with me and you'll eat those words."

"Sunday?" Disappointment reflected in her voice. "Are the drag races held on Sunday?"

"Don't you remember?" he echoed. "That's about the only day all the guys can be sure of gettin' off work or school." He saw the scowl on her face deepen. "What's the matter with Sunday?"

"Dad would never let me go on Sunday," she said lamely.

His laughter was taunting. "I forgot. That dad of yours is as religious as Danny Orlis, isn't he?"

Linda's face flushed hotly. She opened her lips as though to speak but checked herself.

"Your dad wouldn't even need to know where you were," he said. "You could always be going over to a friend's to study or down to the library to read a book for history. They'd never know the difference."

"I–I couldn't do that."

"Why not?" he demanded. "It never used to bother you."

Linda winced. This was her opportunity to give Jack her testimony. She could tell him how much the Lord Jesus Christ meant to her by telling him why she couldn't follow his suggestion. But when she finally spoke, it was not to give her testimony. Instead she directed her attention to the car engine, and said, "It sounds different than it used to, Jack."

"If it didn't sound different, and run different, too," he continued boastfully, "I would sure feel as though I'd got stung." His laughter crescendoed. "I sure spent a lot of my old man's hard-earned cash gettin' her souped up the way I wanted her. She's hotter'n any other car in town." He turned the corner expertly. "I can outrun anything on the road – even those cars the highway patrol are drivin'."

"Their cars aren't any different than any others, are they?" she asked.

"Any different?" he echoed. "They put the best thing the factory makes in those patrol cars. They're fast!"

She looked at him admiringly. "You were just kidding about being able to beat them."

"Kiddin'?" he laughed again, derision curling his lips. "I wouldn't be afraid to take 'em on any day, but they've got their radios to catch a guy. All they've got to do is to radio ahead and put up a roadblock, and you're a dead duck."

Linda sighed her relief. "Maybe it's just as well that we can't go too fast now."

His eyes narrowed suspiciously. "That doesn't sound much like you, Kitten," he retorted. "The truth is, you haven't acted like yourself for quite a while." He drove halfway across town. Then he asked, "Where's the girl who used to be ready for anything?"

She moistened her lips with the tip of her tongue and swallowed hard. "There–there's something I've got to tell you, Jack," she began, fumbling for words.

His eyes narrowed. "Now, what's that?" he demanded irritably.

Linda squirmed. Now that she had begun, she

had to continue. There was no turning back – no changing the subject, but it was so hard to talk to a guy like Jack. He would never understand. "I–I'm different now then I used to be," she said. "I'm different than I've ever been."

"Different?" His voice crescendoed. "That's no name for it, Kitten. It's a good thing I came along to jolt you out of whatever it is that hit you. You act as though you're about to vegetate or something."

Linda flushed hotly. She fought for words, but they would not come. Every now and then Jack would glance in her direction. He was angry at her. She could see that. Angrier than he had ever been before. But he did not continue his questioning. He drove five or six miles north of town, made a U-turn on the highway, and came back.

Before he spoke again, they were nearing the city limits once more. "Let's stop in here and have a bottle of pop before we go home," he said. "How does that suit you?"

Linda started to agree when she saw the brightly lighted beer signs that marked the place as a tavern. She shook her head. "I–I'd like a bottle of pop," she told him, "but I certainly don't want to go into a place like that to get it."

Jack Ross paid no attention to her protest. Expertly he braked the car and pulled into the parking lot. "That's just because you haven't been around. You go into a place like this a few times and you'll see what it's like." Then his tone of voice changed, and he begged, "Come on, Kitten, this is a swell place."

"But–" she began.

"Just because we go in here is no sign that we have to have a drink. All I want is a bottle of pop."

Reluctantly Linda got out of the car, and they started toward the dimly lit building. A few paces from the door she stopped. The sign proclaimed boldly, No Minors Allowed.

"We can't go in there, Jack," she said, relief in her voice. "We're not old enough."

He laughed indulgently. "Don't let that sign throw you. It's only there because the cops made them put it there. Me and my friends have been going here for weeks. That little old sign doesn't mean a thing." He took her by the arm and started forward. "Come on, Kitten, don't be so disagreeable."

At that moment a car went slowly by. The girl turned, her face going ashen. "Oh, Jack!" she cried in dismay.

"Now, what's the matter?"

"That woman who just went by is a good friend of Elsie's! Now I'm in for it!"

* * *

Linda Penner remained motionless in the tavern parking lot, staring at the taillights of the car that was moving slowly down the road. Jack Ross turned back to her, disgust darkening his eyes. "Now, what's wrong with you this time?" he asked.

"That woman who just went by is a good friend of Elsie's, and she saw me! *I know she did!*"

"What's so terrible about that? You haven't done anything so bad."

"Elsie's the woman who married my dad," Linda continued. "Her friend will tell her, and she'll tell Dad, and I'll be in real trouble!"

Jack Ross snorted in disdain. "I wouldn't get so upset about it if I were you. Come on in and have a bottle of pop with me. I've had a lot of experience in squirming out of deals like this. We'll think of something to get out of this."

Linda shook her head. "You can go in if you want to, Jack," she said, her voice trembling with emotion. "I'll wait for you in the car."

"Now, what kind of a deal is that?"

"I can't go in there with you," she repeated. "That's all there is to it. You go on in and I–I'll wait for you."

He stared at her as though he could not quite believe what she was saying. "You sure turned out to be a killjoy tonight!" he exploded. "I'm beginning to believe that the story I've been hearing about you is true. You do sound as though you've got religion."

Linda took a deep breath. Regardless of what happened she couldn't postpone talking to Jack any longer. She had to tell him that she had trusted the Lord Jesus Christ as her Savior and was striving to live for Him!

"How about it?" he snarled angrily, "are you going inside with me or are you going to ruin the whole evening for both of us?"

"I–I should have told you this before," she said hesitantly, "but I–I'm a Christian now, Jack."

His eyes widened incredulously.

"The story you heard is true," she continued. "I–I accepted Christ as my Savior over at Mrs. Orlis's house a few weeks ago."

Jack Ross shook his head. "If you weren't telling me this yourself, I wouldn't believe it," he answered. "I just wouldn't believe it!"

"Being a Christian is–is not like you think it is at all, Jack," she said defensively. "It's–"

But he wasn't listening to her. He had already turned and was storming back to the car.

"Come on!" he ordered hotly, "if you want a ride home, you'd better get in before I change my mind. I just might go off and leave you."

She got into the seat beside him and sat there, very still and quiet. This wasn't the way she had planned it at all. She had worked out a way of giving him her testimony to which she thought he would listen. She had decided just how she would go about telling him how good it was to know that Christ had saved her from sin, and how much happier she had been since she had made a decision for the Lord. But somehow it wasn't working out as she had planned. Once or twice her lips parted as though to speak, but her voice choked off. Jack glanced at her a time or two but said nothing.

In front of the Penner home, he braked the car to a stop. Reaching for the car door handle, Linda paused and turned to face him. "I–I'm sorry, Jack," she said.

"Skip it."

"It's not the way you think it is at all!"

"You've decided which is the most important to you, Linda. That's okay. I know when I'm licked." His lips curled bitterly. "You want this stupid religion of yours more than you want to go out with me – so, okay. That's the way it's goin' to be! But just remember! You and I are done! Finished!"

She got out of the car, feeling weak, and as he slammed the door behind her, she heard him say, "I'm sorry I wasted my time on you!"

CHAPTER 9

LINDA'S NEW MOTHER IS "IN"

She walked slowly up the walk to the front door. Her face was pallid, and her hands and shoulders were trembling, she knew, but there was nothing she could do about it.

Her dad and Elsie were sitting in the living room listening to music and reading when she came in. Henry looked up, and said, "Hey, you are home early. I didn't expect you for at least twenty minutes."

"I–I didn't stay quite as long as I thought I would," she told him.

He glanced down at the paper once more. For a moment or two Linda stood there, looking from one to the other, as though undecided whether to talk with them or not. "Elsie," she began, "did–did Mrs. Martin call you a little while ago?"

Elsie Penner's forehead crinkled questionably. "Mrs. Martin?" she asked. "Do you mean Lulu Martin?"

The girl nodded.

"I don't think she would have anything to be calling about. I was with her for a while this afternoon."

Linda took off her coat and sat down. Her hands were working nervously.

"Is something wrong?" the older woman asked.

Linda did not answer immediately, but when she did her voice was taut.

"I–I've got something that I–I've got to tell you," she began.

"Yes?" Elsie spoke gently.

Henry Penner closed his book and laid it aside.

"I–I told you that I was going down to the snack shop." Once the words began to come out, they tumbled with a rush. "But I–I–"

"Are you trying to tell us that you didn't go to the shop this evening, Linda," he said, "after you told us that was where you were going?" Henry Penner's voice was gentle but stern.

Linda continued quickly. "Oh, I went to the shop, all right," she told him. "But I–I didn't go to stay there. I mean, I went there to meet Jack Ross."

Her dad uncrossed his legs and sat up. Anger and disappointment deepened the lines in his face. "Jack Ross?" he echoed. "Is that the Ross boy who has gotten into so much trouble the last couple of years?"

Linda's face was white and drawn, but she did not hesitate or try to make excuses for herself. "He–he's the one. I–I hate to have to tell you this, Daddy, but I–I've been dating Jack Ross for the past few months."

Henry Penner stiffened. "I think I remember distinctly that I told you not to go out with Jack Ross or anyone else with a reputation like his."

"I know you did."

"And you deliberately disobeyed me!"

"I deliberately disobeyed you," she admitted, "but please, Daddy, let me explain." But she found it hard to begin.

Finally Mr. Penner broke the silence. "I'm waiting," he said icily.

"I–I wanted to talk with him and tell him that I had trusted Christ as my Savior," she said. "I wanted to explain that I couldn't go out with him anymore because I was a Christian and he wasn't. That was the only reason I agreed to go with him in the first place. But when I tried to see him at school, I couldn't manage it. So I–I went down to the shop to meet him."

"And you went out with him in his car after I told you that you couldn't go out with him anymore."

Her eyes pleaded with him. "I tried to get him to talk to me in the snack shop, but he wouldn't talk there. He wanted to show me his car." Hesitantly she told them everything that had taken place that evening. Neither Elsie nor Henry interrupted her until she had finished. "I'm awfully sorry," she concluded at last. "Really I am. I didn't mean to do it. I mean, I–I'm sorry that I deceived you and everything."

Elsie spoke up quickly. "I know you did the wrong thing this evening, Linda. There isn't any question about that. You should have told us who you were meeting and asked our permission. But I'm so glad that you came to us the way you have. It shows that you are really concerned about living a holy Christian life, also that you want to make things right when you have done wrong."

"I wouldn't even have gotten into the car with Jack if I'd known he was going to stop at that bar," Linda said.

"That's the way it is with sin," Elsie said. "We put ourselves into positions of temptation and don't even realize what has happened until it's too late."

"I tried to get Jack to go somewhere else," Linda continued, "but he just laughed at me and kept insisting that I go in with him and see how nice it was and how much fun we'd have there. It wasn't until I told him that I now am a Christian that he brought me home." Her voice cracked. "And he was so mad at me that I know I'm never going to have to worry about him asking me to go anywhere again." Her eyes brimmed with tears. "You do believe me, don't you?"

Mr. Penner hesitated, but Elsie nodded quickly. "I'm sure that you're telling us the way things actually happened, Linda. And I'm sure that you're sorry for what you did and have been doing."

Linda looked up at her gratefully. "Oh, I am."

Mr. Penner talked with her for a few minutes and then left the room. Elsie wanted to talk more with

Linda, so she remained where she was. "I want to tell you how glad I am that you came directly to us and confessed, Linda," she said in soft tones. "That was very difficult for you, I know."

The girl's eyes met hers. "Mrs. Martin would probably have told you anyway."

"That doesn't matter. As long as you have told us because you are sorry for what you did and want to ask our forgiveness, I am very, very happy."

Linda was silent for a few moments. Then she said, "I don't think I'll have to worry about Jack Ross anymore. He's so mad at me now that–that I don't suppose he'll ever speak to me again."

"I would like to talk to you about Jack, Linda, and the other boys like Jack that you'll be meeting as you get older. Some of them are very nice boys – even if they are unsaved, I mean. And you'll likely want to date some of them. But, Linda, dear, the Bible warns very specifically against it."

Linda nodded soberly. "That's what Kay told me." She took a deep breath. "But I didn't pay any attention to her at first. I thought I would be able to tell Jack about Christ. Then when I did think about the fact that I shouldn't be going with him, it was too late. I'd already told him that I would."

"I understand just how it was," Elsie went on. "And I don't mean to criticize you. I did the same thing when I was a girl. You know, a lot of girls get the idea that if they keep going with their unsaved boyfriends, they'll be able to lead them to Christ, but it usually doesn't work out that way. For every girl who's able to lead a boyfriend to Christ, there are a hundred or more who try and don't succeed." She spoke slowly. "The only way that you can be sure you are going to fall in love with a Christian young man and have a Christian home and family is to date only those who are Christians."

"But Elsie," Linda protested, "there are so few Christian guys at school! If I didn't go with non-Christian boys, I never would have a date." Her voice softened slightly. "Besides, I don't plan on marrying a guy just because I happen to have a couple of dates with him."

"You may think that to refuse to date unsaved boys is a big sacrifice now, but in a few years, when you have graduated from high school and have found a fine Christian young man whom you really love with all your heart, you'll be glad you waited."

They talked on for half an hour or more. When they finally finished, Linda rose and went to the bedroom she shared with Becky. After she got into bed, she lay there thinking what a grand person Elsie was. She wasn't anything like Linda had thought she was going to be. Why, Elsie was kind and understanding and she really did care about Becky and her. If Elsie didn't care, it wouldn't make the slightest difference to her who Linda dated or what time she got in or anything.

A smile lit Linda's young face. Maybe it wasn't going to be so bad having Elsie around after all.

The next morning at school Linda was just taking off her coat to hang it in her locker when Jack Ross came up to her. "Hi, Kitten."

She glanced back at him. "Hello."

"Still mad at me?"

"I never was mad at you. You were the one who was mad. Remember?"

He shrugged his shoulders. "That's all over now. We were sure lucky last night!"

"What do you mean?"

"We were lucky we didn't go into that bar. That's what I stopped to tell you."

She turned to face him, questions lighting her eyes.

"Didn't you hear what happened?" he asked guardedly. "The police raided the tavern where we stopped about ten minutes after we drove out. They picked up half a dozen high school kids and took them down to the police station. Some of them were booked for drinking and the cops made their parents come down after the rest of them." He took a deep breath and slowly exhaled. "If my old man had gotten a phone call like that, I'd be grounded for a year." His smile was spontaneous. "I sure do owe you a lot."

Linda smiled slowly.

If it hadn't been for Elsie, she would have been in bad trouble herself. She really owed her a lot.

"I guess we have to thank my new mother," she said, using a tone in speaking of Elsie that she had never used before.

THE DANNY ORLIS SERIES

The Danny Orlis series, by Bernard Palmer, delivers a blend of adventure, mystery, and suspense through various settings—from the Canadian wilderness to Guatemalan jungles. Danny Orlis, an adept outdoorsman, skilled athlete, and committed Christian, employs his quick thinking, calm bravery, and biblical solutions to confront everyday problems and hair-raising dangers. Early stories focus on Danny navigating school life, sports, and outdoor challenges, while in later books, Danny and his wife Kay provide wisdom and guidance to youngsters facing lifelike situations and challenges. Having sold over two million copies, this series has made Palmer a renowned author in Christian youth literature. Palmer is also the author of the Felicia Cartright series and various other series for Christian youth.

AVAILABLE FROM WWW.ANEKOPRESS.COM